~~CAPTAIN EPIC: DAWN OF AWESOMENESS~~

~~THE LEGEND OF SMARTACUS~~

SUPER DWEEB V
DOCTOR ERASER-BUTT

By Jess Bradley

So, we're definitely going with "Super Dweeb," huh?

Would you rather have "butt" in your name?

NO!

ARCTURUS

NO, TATER-TOT! THAT'S NOT A TOY!

ARCTURUS

This edition published in 2021 by Arcturus
Publishing Limited, 26/27 Bickels Yard, 151–153
Bermondsey Street, London SE1 3HA

Words and pictures: Jess Bradley
Design: Stefan Holliland
Original concept: Joe Harris
Art direction: Rosie Bellwood

ISBN: 978-1-3988-0246-9
CH007612NT
Supplier 13, Date 0521, Print run 10767

Printed in China

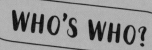

WHO'S WHO?

ANDY! Schoolkid and secret superhero

Awesome rating: <u>THE AWESOMEST</u>

MONA! Andy's best friend and tech genius

Awesome rating: <u>ELEVEN OUT OF TEN</u>

OSCAR! Andy's annoying little brother

Awesome rating: <u>NOT VERY</u>

MEAN MIKE! A school bully

Awesome rating: <u>THE EXACT OPPOSITE OF AWESOME</u>

THE PENCIL OF DESTINY!

A radioactive pencil that can bring doodles to life!

Awesome rating: <u>OFF THE SCALE</u>

CONTENTS

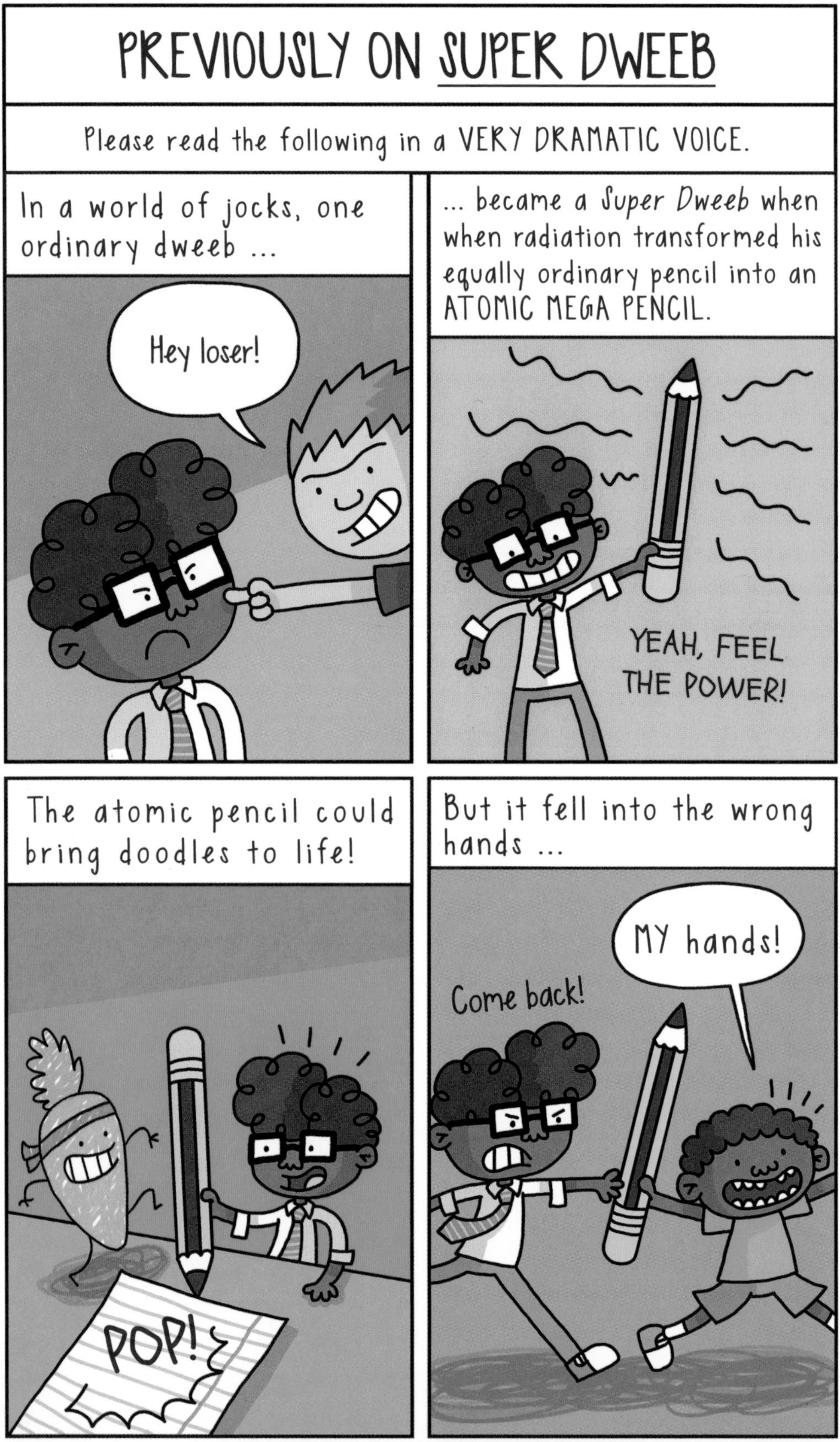
PREVIOUSLY ON SUPER DWEEB
Please read the following in a VERY DRAMATIC VOICE.
In a world of jocks, one ordinary dweeb ...
Hey loser!
... became a Super Dweeb when when radiation transformed his equally ordinary pencil into an ATOMIC MEGA PENCIL.
YEAH, FEEL THE POWER!
The atomic pencil could bring doodles to life!
POP!
But it fell into the wrong hands ...
Come back!
MY hands!

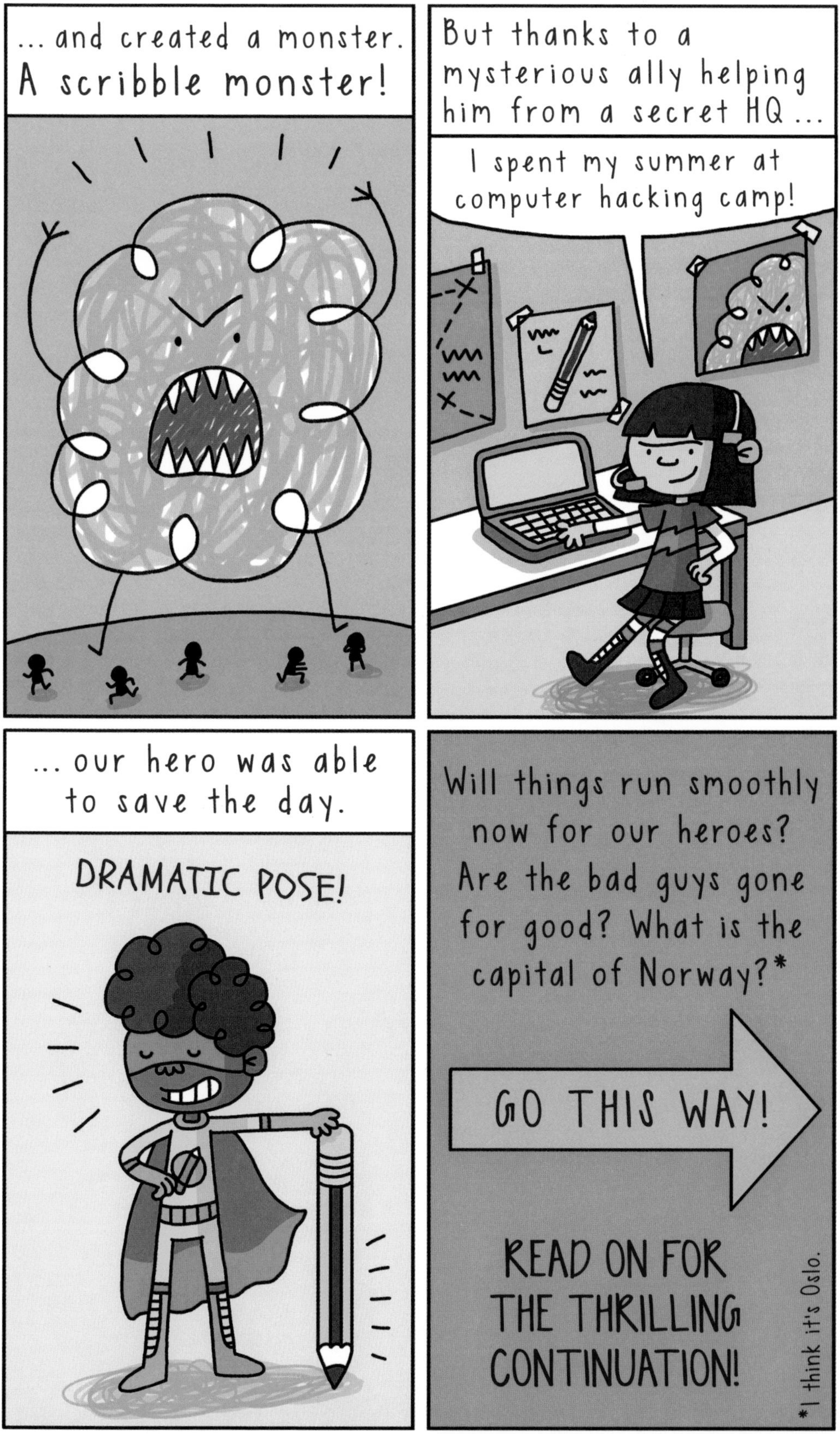
... and created a monster. A scribble monster!
But thanks to a mysterious ally helping him from a secret HQ ...
I spent my summer at computer hacking camp!
... our hero was able to save the day.
DRAMATIC POSE!
Will things run smoothly now for our heroes? Are the bad guys gone for good? What is the capital of Norway?*
GO THIS WAY!
READ ON FOR THE THRILLING CONTINUATION!
*I think it's Oslo.

Chapter 1 Dweeb Life

Hey there, I'm ANDY. Here's a picture of me looking like I just had A REALLY GREAT IDEA!

Everyone says that I'm a massive DWEEB—but my best friend MONA says that being a dweeb is AWESOME, and that I "totally own it."

Here are some things you should know about me!

—I like making my own COMIC BOOKS.

—Yes, I wear a tie. Yes, it's on purpose.

—I have a near-complete set of of GAMMA GUYS trading cards. I'm just missing Roid-zilla™. Let me know if you have a spare!

Oh, and I'm a SECRET SUPERHERO. Maybe I should have led with that. This is me in my costume.

Ever since I became a superhero, I've had a lot on my plate.

MY "TO-DO" LIST:

FIGHT BAD GUYS!

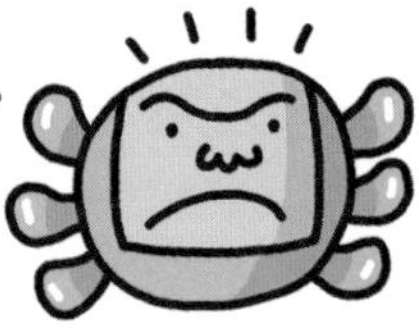

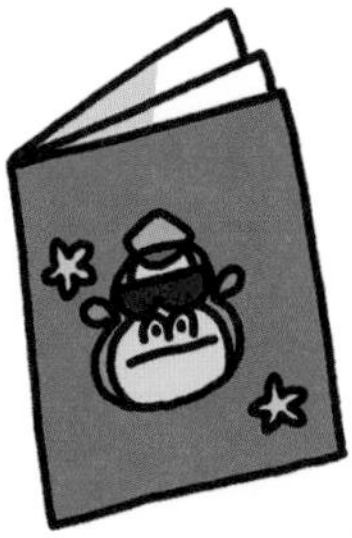

DRAW AWESOME COMICS!

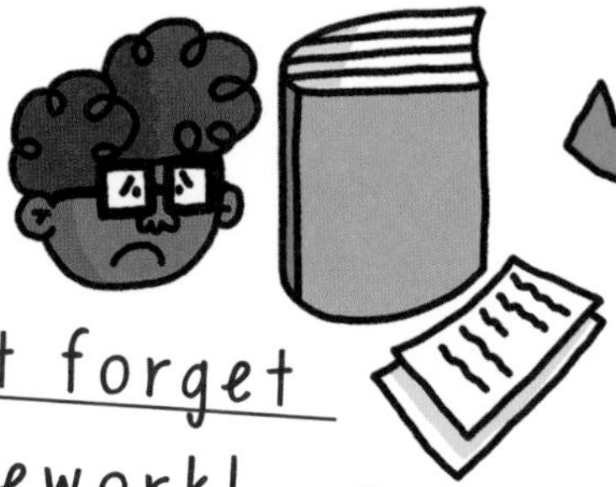

Don't forget homework!

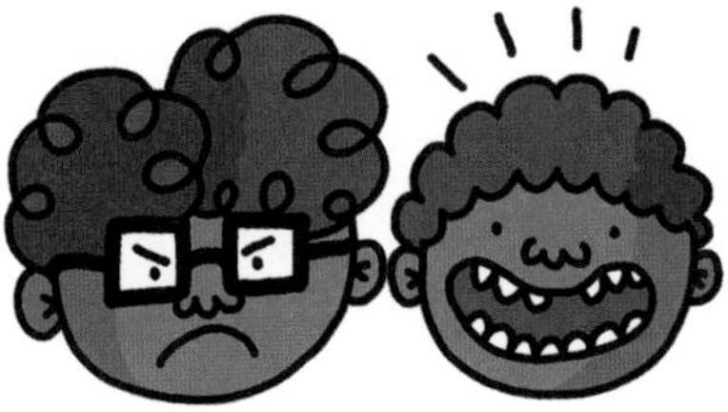

LOOK AFTER OSCAR (MY LITTLE BROTHER)!

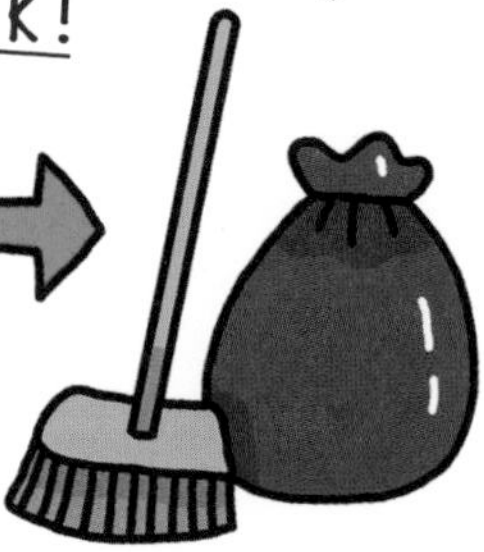

DO CHORES!

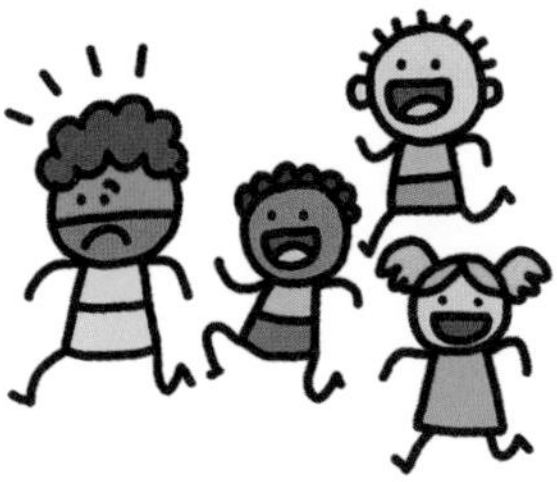

DEAL WITH FANS!

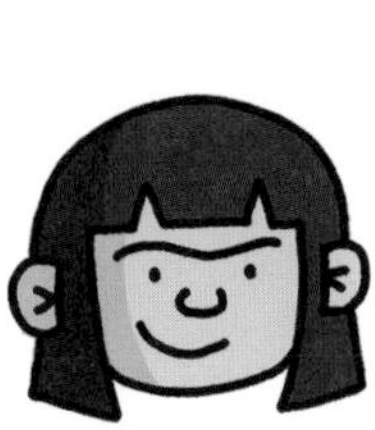

Hang out with my best friend!

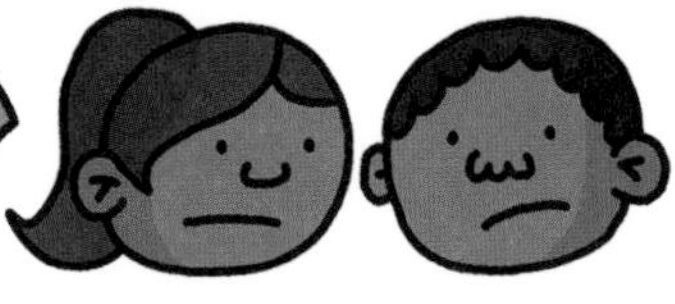

Make sure Mom and Dad don't find out about the whole SUPERHERO thing!

It's hard to juggle so much important stuff. Fortunately, I've came up with a sneaky solution! Before I go out crime fighting, I doodle a picture of myself.

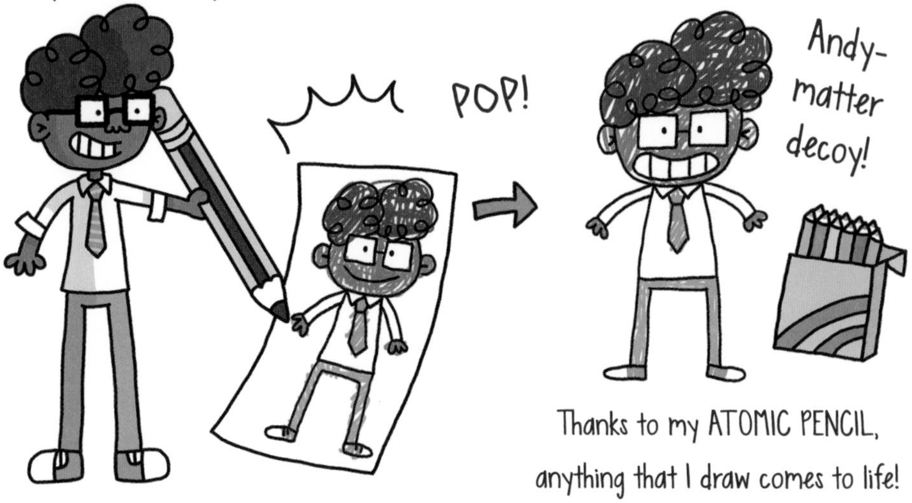
POP!
Andy-matter decoy!

Thanks to my ATOMIC PENCIL, anything that I draw comes to life!

Normally my living doodles only last ten minutes, but my "Andy-matter decoys" can live longer by eating normal pencils.

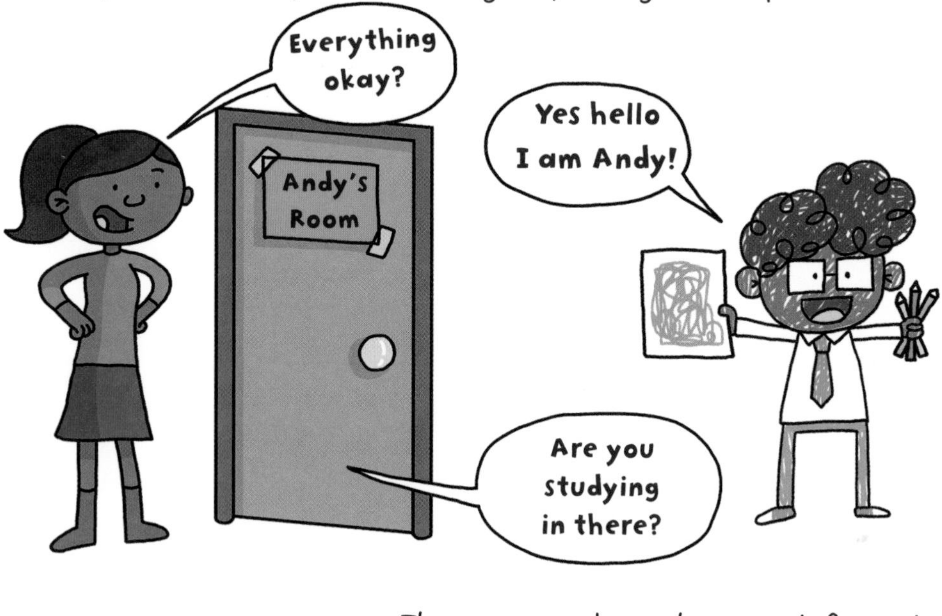
Everything okay?
Andy's Room
Yes hello I am Andy!
Are you studying in there?

They can even do my homework for me!

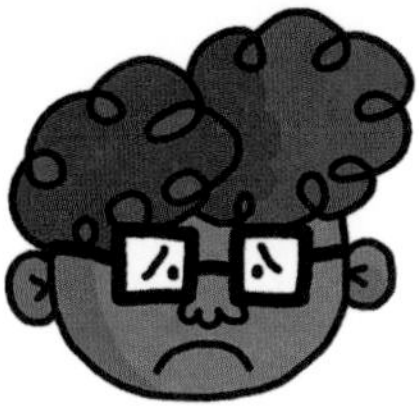

Of course, I feel pretty lousy about lying to my parents but it's all for the greater good, right? So far, I'm doing okay keeping everything in line. Now the only thing I **REALLY** need to do is get home before my parents read my ...

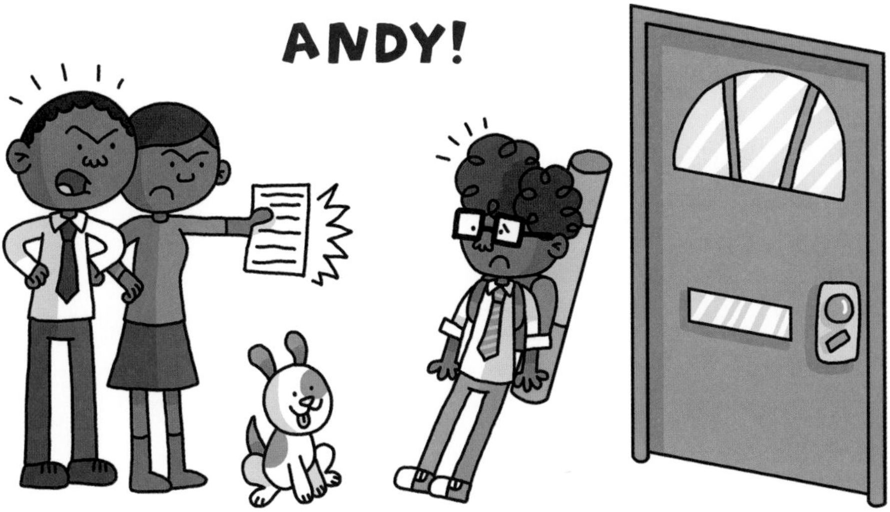
ANDY!

... report card. GULP!

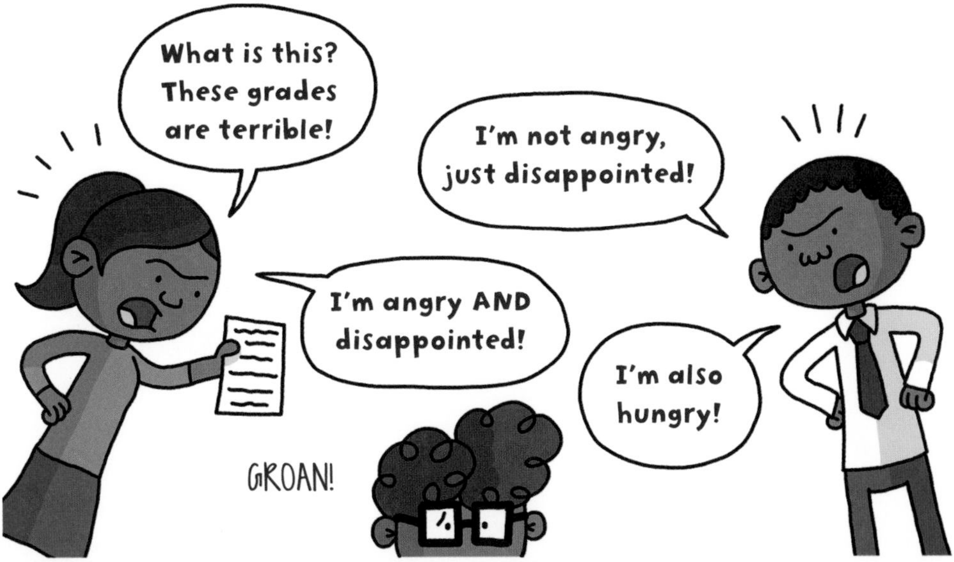
What is this? These grades are terrible!
I'm not angry, just disappointed!
I'm angry AND disappointed!
I'm also hungry!
GROAN!

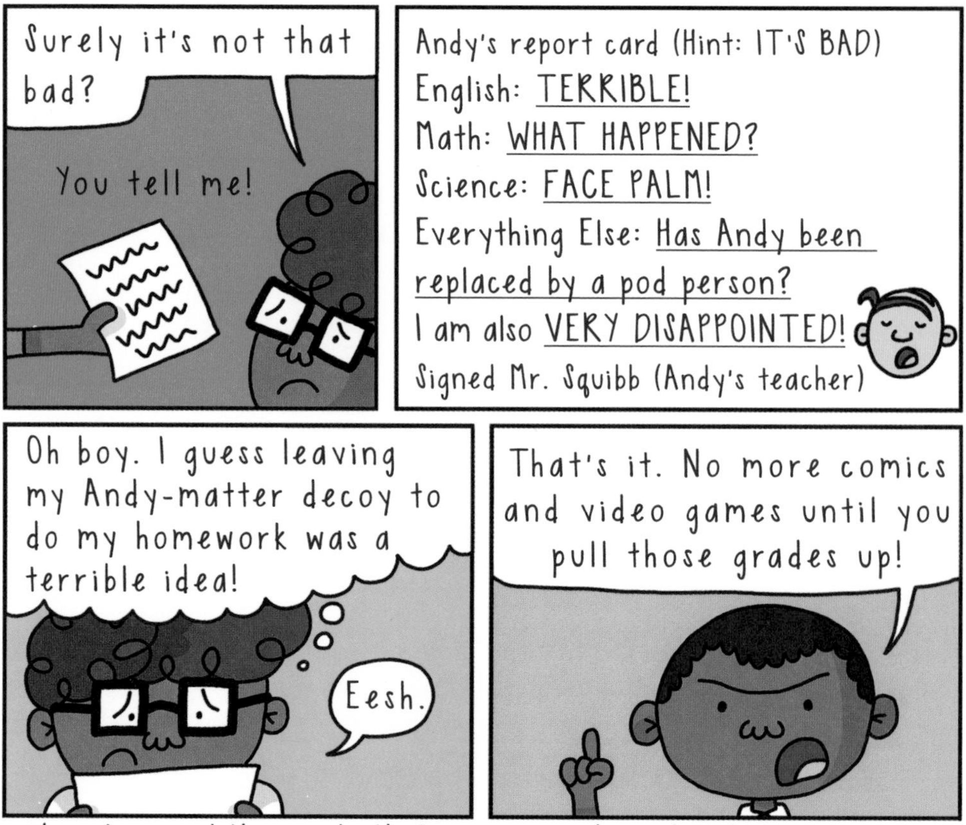
Surely it's not that bad?
You tell me!
Andy's report card (Hint: IT'S BAD)
English: TERRIBLE!
Math: WHAT HAPPENED?
Science: FACE PALM!
Everything Else: Has Andy been replaced by a pod person?
I am also VERY DISAPPOINTED!
Signed Mr. Squibb (Andy's teacher)
Oh boy. I guess leaving my Andy-matter decoy to do my homework was a terrible idea!
Eesh.
That's it. No more comics and video games until you pull those grades up!

Then Mom said the words that every superhero dreads:

"If you don't pass the big test tomorrow, you'll be GROUNDED!"

"Nooo!" I cried. "But I can't be grounded! I need to, uh..."

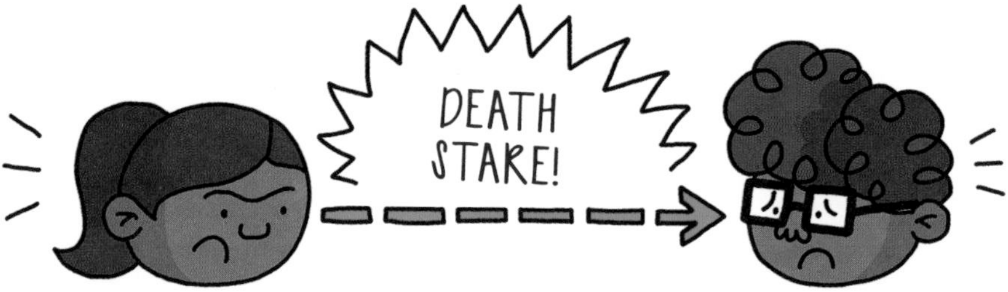
DEATH STARE!

I sighed. "I guess I'll go study." I went upstairs to my room.

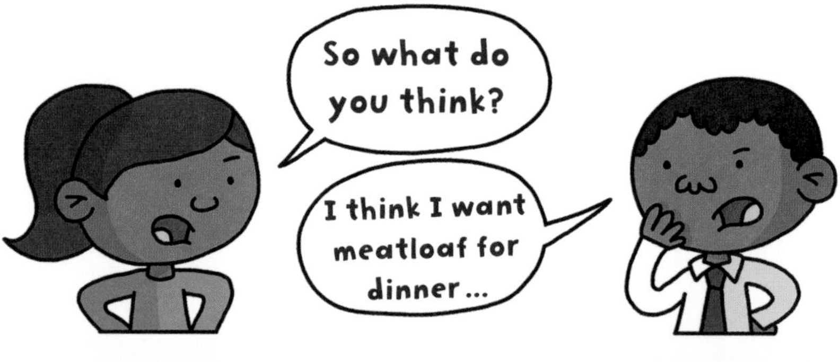
So what do you think?
I think I want meatloaf for dinner...

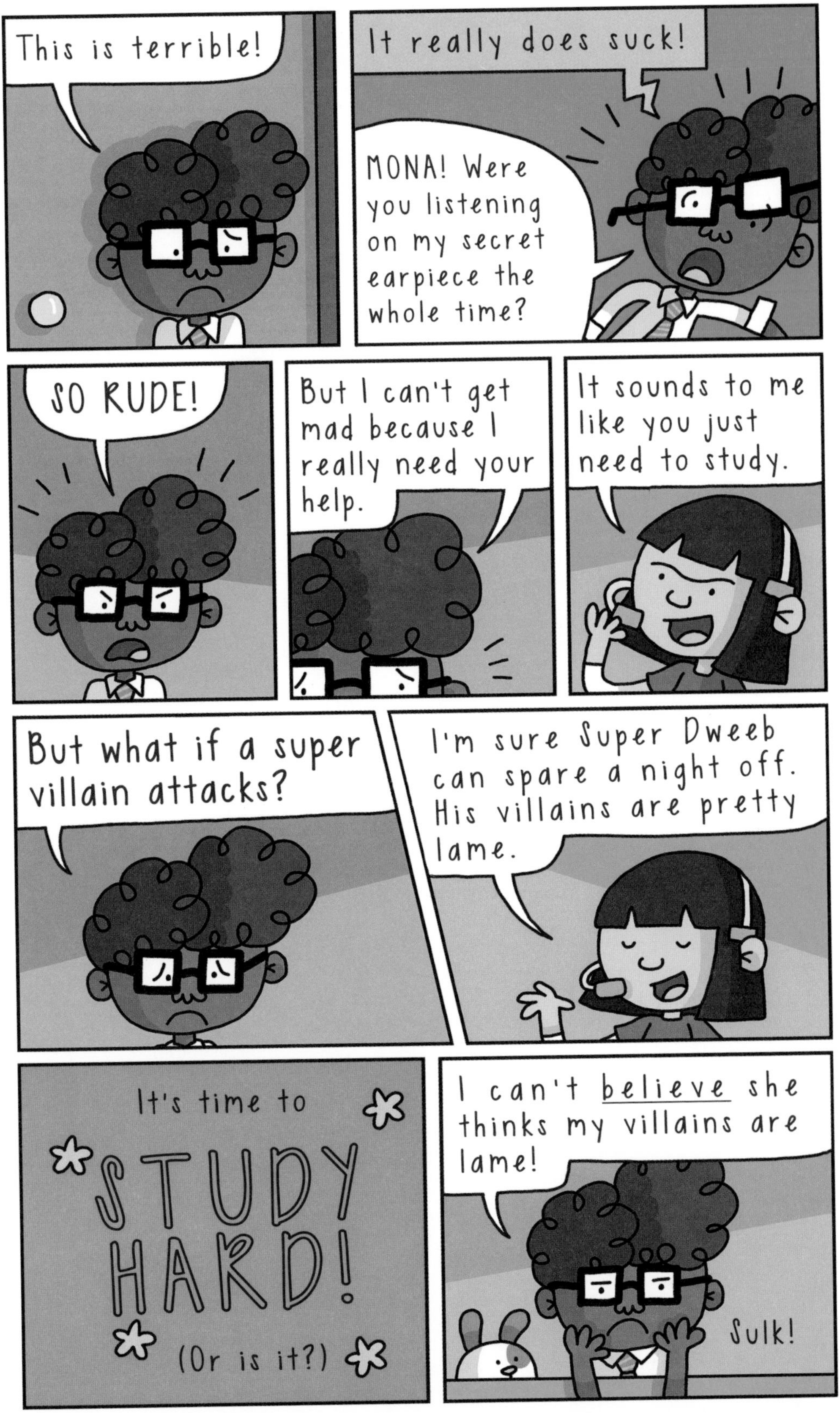
This is terrible!
It really does suck!
MONA! Were you listening on my secret earpiece the whole time?
SO RUDE!
But I can't get mad because I really need your help.
It sounds to me like you just need to study.
But what if a super villain attacks?
I'm sure Super Dweeb can spare a night off. His villains are pretty lame.
It's time to
STUDY HARD!
(Or is it?)
I can't believe she thinks my villains are lame!
Sulk!

Chapter 2 **Sinister Super Spy Squad**

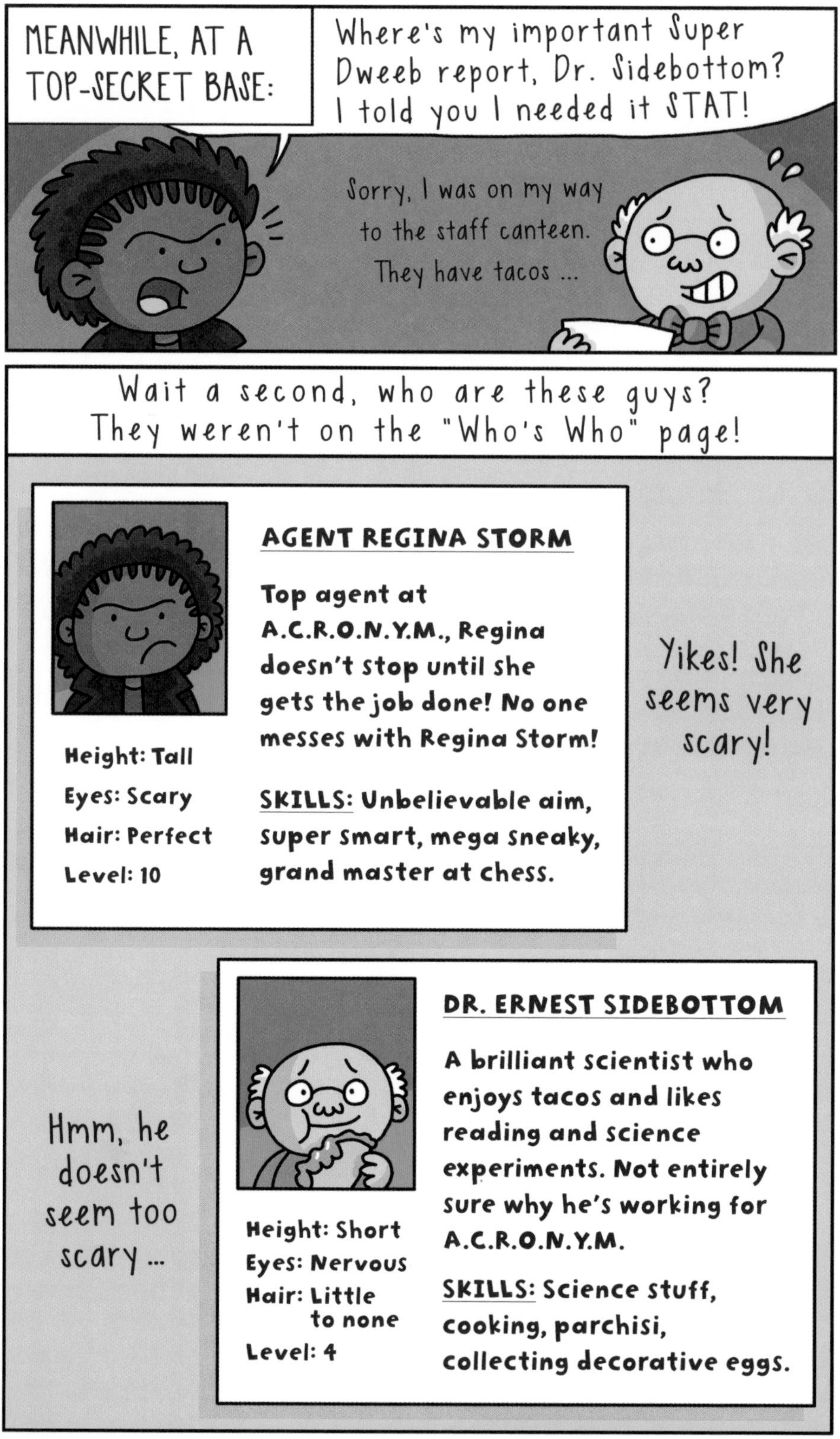
MEANWHILE, AT A TOP-SECRET BASE:
Where's my important Super Dweeb report, Dr. Sidebottom? I told you I needed it STAT!
Sorry, I was on my way to the staff canteen. They have tacos ...
Wait a second, who are these guys? They weren't on the "Who's Who" page!
AGENT REGINA STORM
Top agent at A.C.R.O.N.Y.M., Regina doesn't stop until she gets the job done! No one messes with Regina Storm!
Height: Tall
Eyes: Scary
Hair: Perfect
Level: 10
SKILLS: Unbelievable aim, super smart, mega sneaky, grand master at chess.
Yikes! She seems very scary!
DR. ERNEST SIDEBOTTOM
A brilliant scientist who enjoys tacos and likes reading and science experiments. Not entirely sure why he's working for A.C.R.O.N.Y.M.
Height: Short
Eyes: Nervous
Hair: Little to none
Level: 4
SKILLS: Science stuff, cooking, parchisi, collecting decorative eggs.
Hmm, he doesn't seem too scary ...

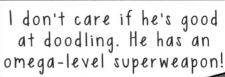

Your report PROVES that the atomic pencil is wasted on that kid.

I think he's pretty a pretty talented artist, though!

I don't care if he's good at doodling. He has an omega-level superweapon!

And you had tacos for lunch yesterday!

But I want tacos every day!

You're an agent of A.C.R.O.N.Y.M. now, Doc! Act like it!

That's enough paperwork. Now it's ACTION TIME! Get in the car.

We're going to find Super Dweeb RIGHT NOW, get a sample, and harness the pencil's power.

VROOM!

Super Dweeb is chasing a bad guy...

Come back!

No way!

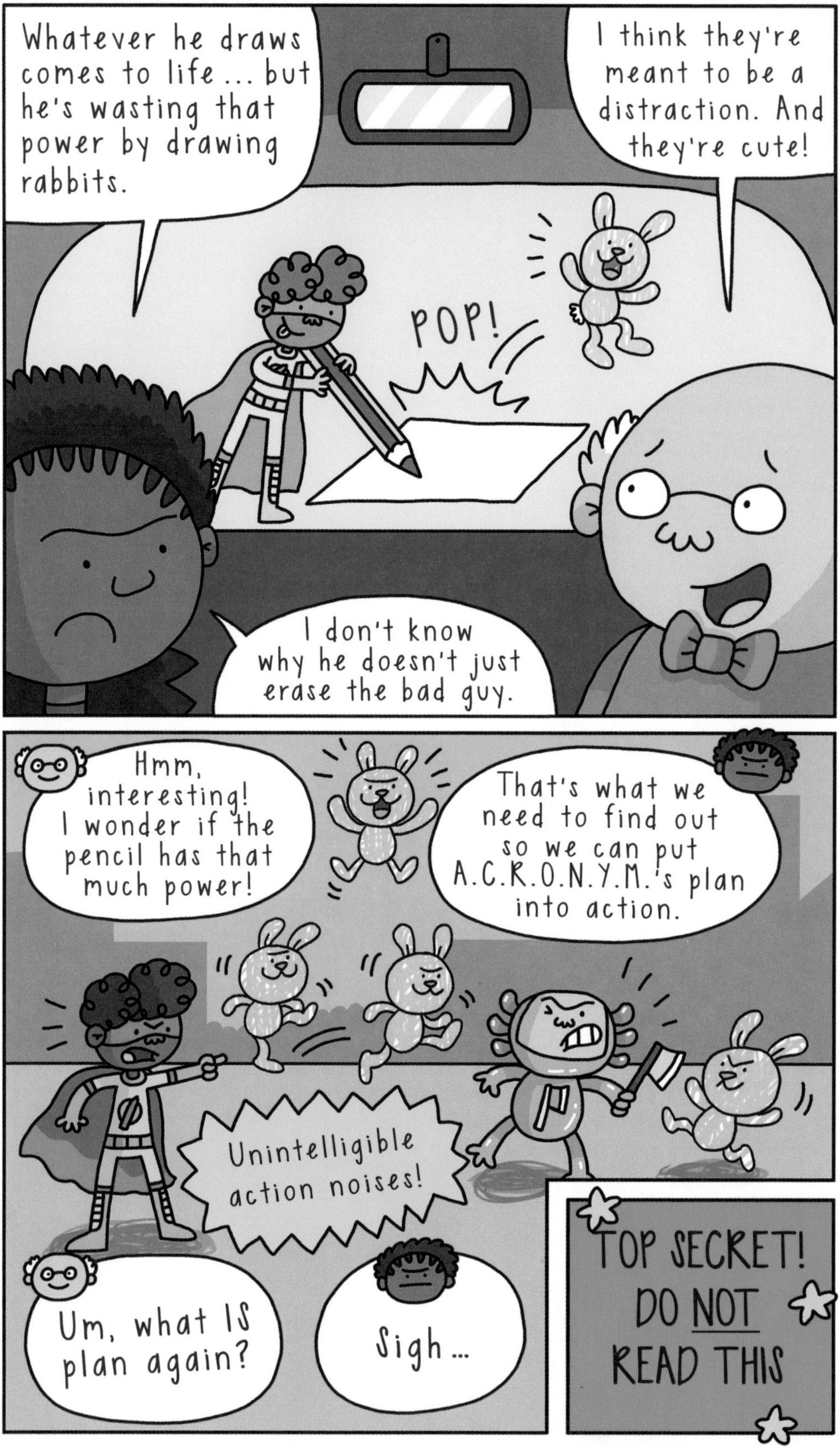
Whatever he draws comes to life ... but he's wasting that power by drawing rabbits.
I think they're meant to be a distraction. And they're cute!
POP!
I don't know why he doesn't just erase the bad guy.
Hmm, interesting! I wonder if the pencil has that much power!
That's what we need to find out so we can put A.C.R.O.N.Y.M.'s plan into action.
Unintelligible action noises!
Um, what IS plan again?
Sigh ...
TOP SECRET! DO NOT READ THIS

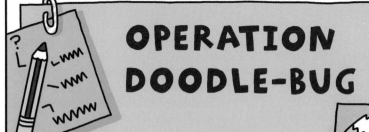

OPERATION DOODLE-BUG

1. Acquire sample of pencil.

2. Make more pencils.

3. Build an army of cybernetic pencil cops to keep the world in check. **No more crime!**

THE POSSIBILITIES ARE ENDLESS!

What is this doing in the file?

Oh, I tried designing my own robot!

Yours is better! Drawing was never my forte!

Sigh.

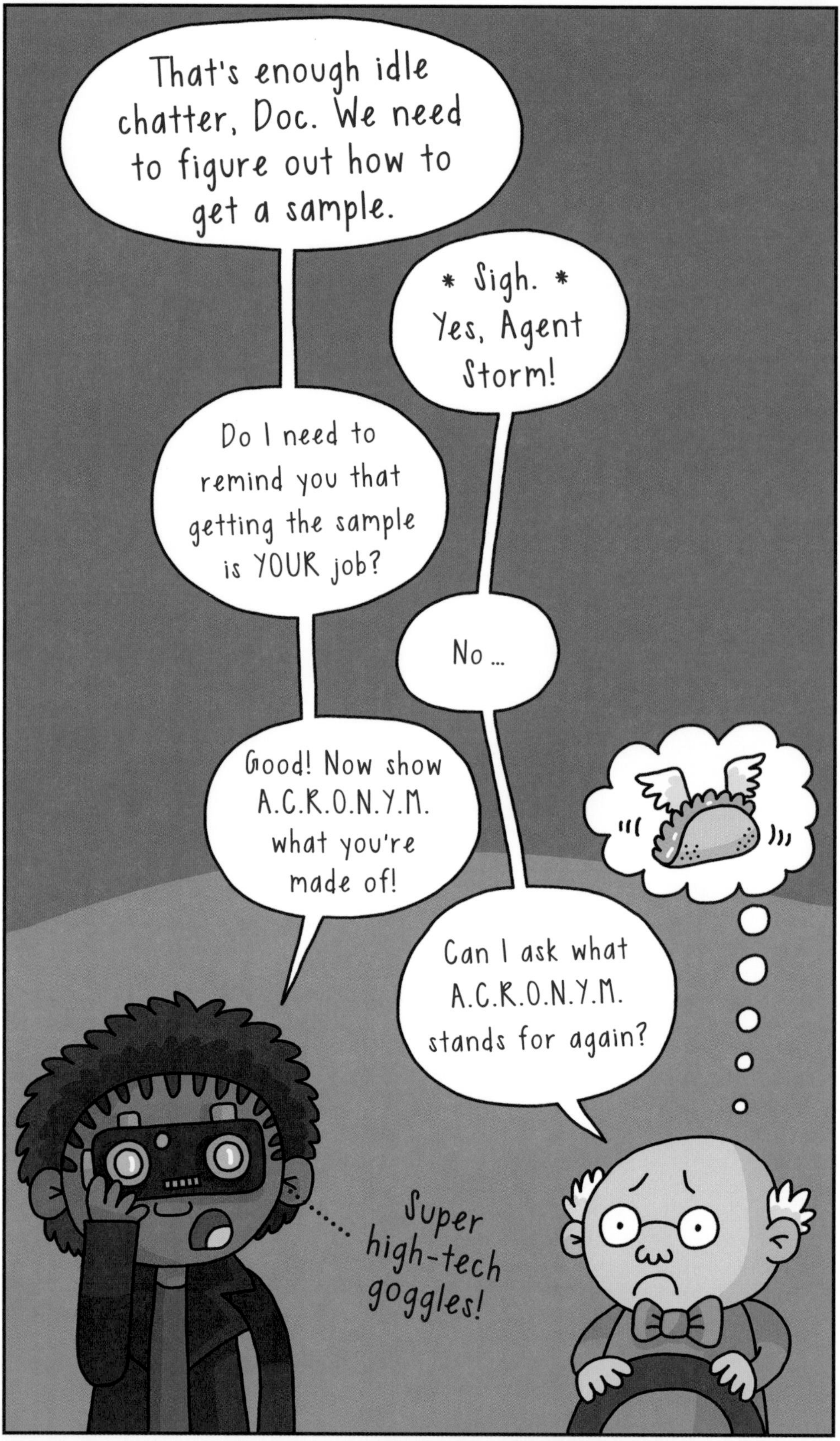
That's enough idle chatter, Doc. We need to figure out how to get a sample.
* Sigh. * Yes, Agent Storm!
Do I need to remind you that getting the sample is YOUR job?
No ...
Good! Now show A.C.R.O.N.Y.M. what you're made of!
Can I ask what A.C.R.O.N.Y.M. stands for again?
Super high-tech goggles!

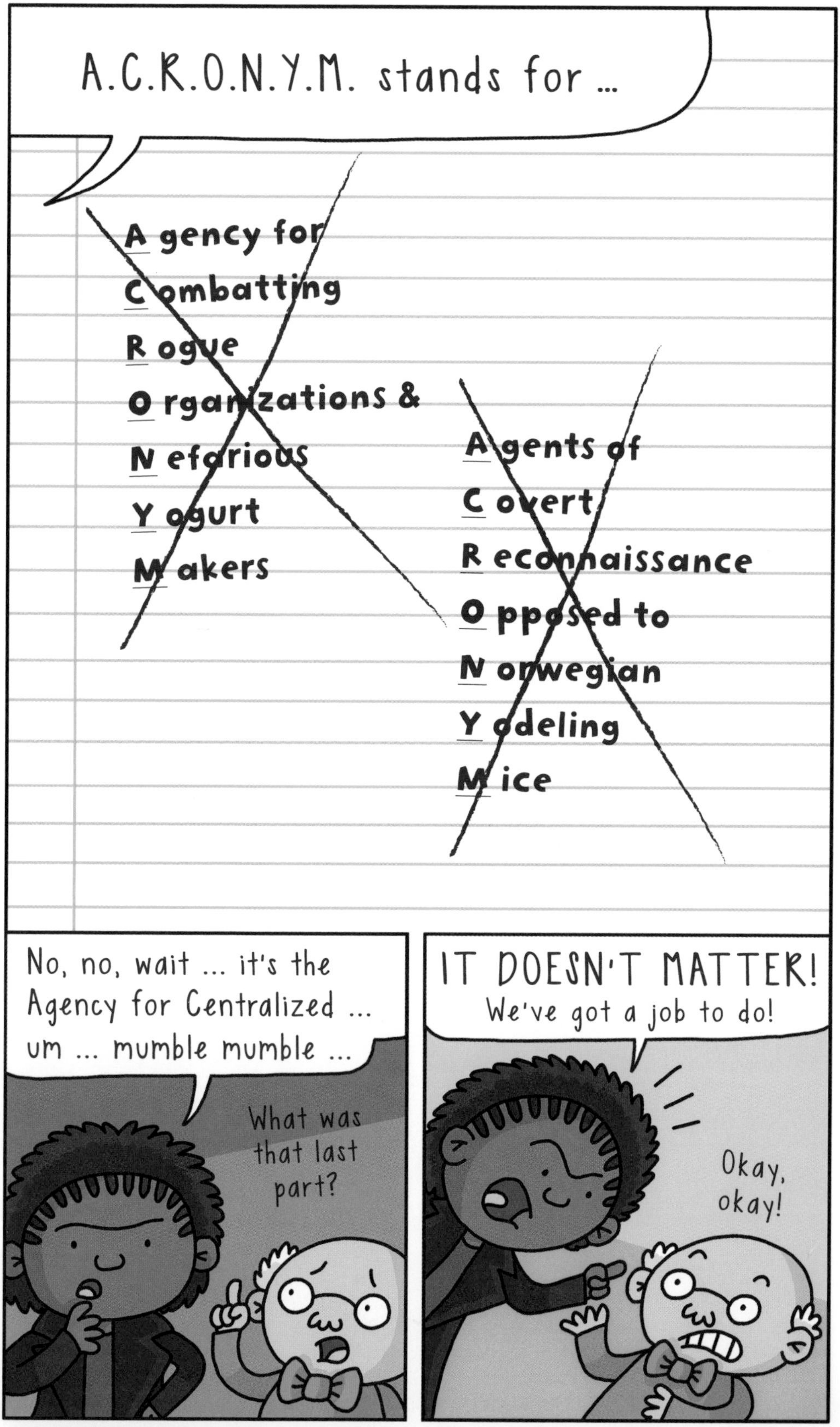
A.C.R.O.N.Y.M. stands for ...
Agency for Combatting Rogue Organizations & Nefarious Yogurt Makers
Agents of Covert Reconnaissance Opposed to Norwegian Yodeling Mice
No, no, wait ... it's the Agency for Centralized ... um ... mumble mumble ...
What was that last part?
IT DOESN'T MATTER! We've got a job to do!
Okay, okay!

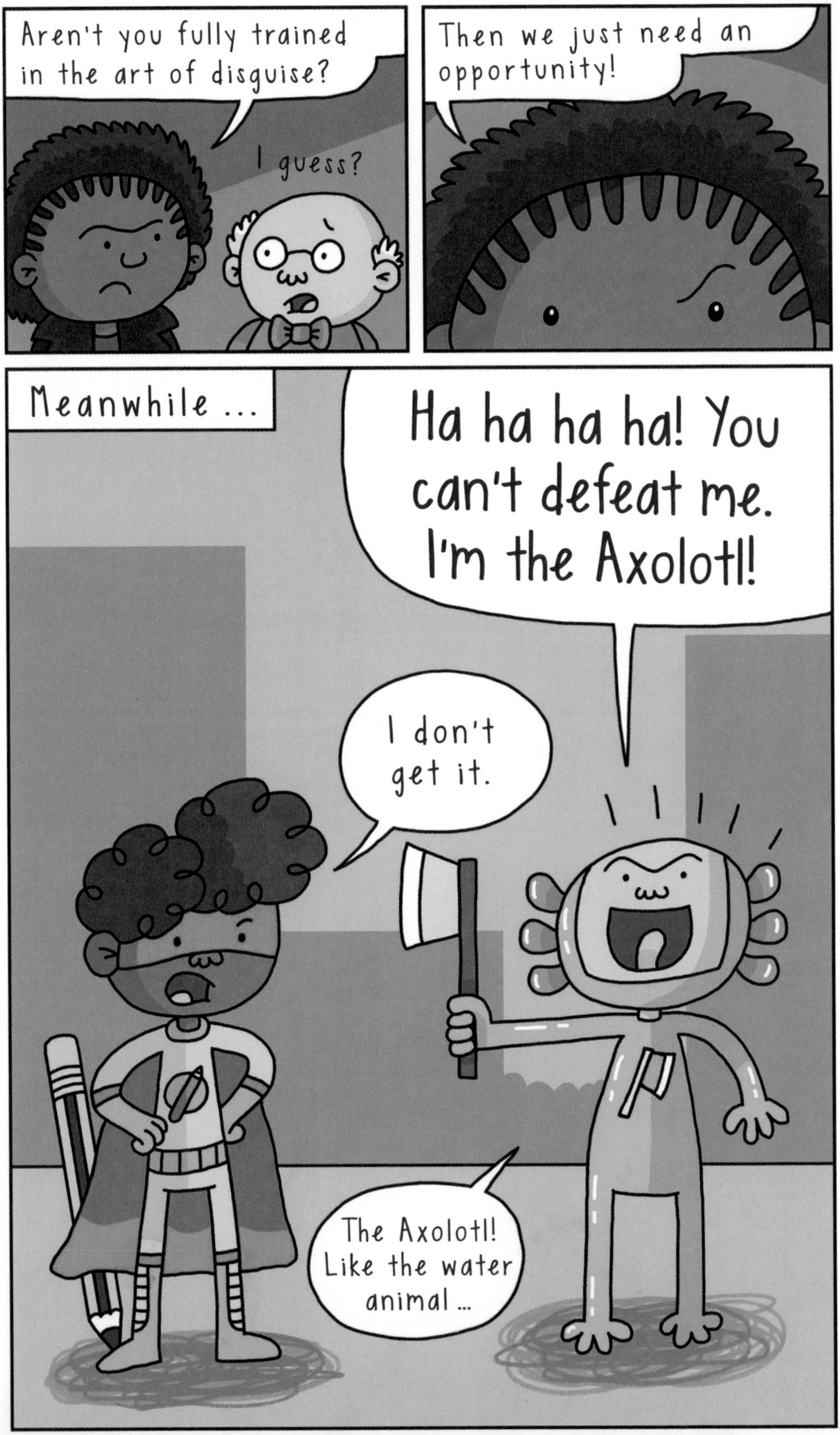
Aren't you fully trained in the art of disguise?
I guess?
Then we just need an opportunity!
Meanwhile ...
Ha ha ha ha! You can't defeat me. I'm the Axolotl!
I don't get it.
The Axolotl! Like the water animal ...

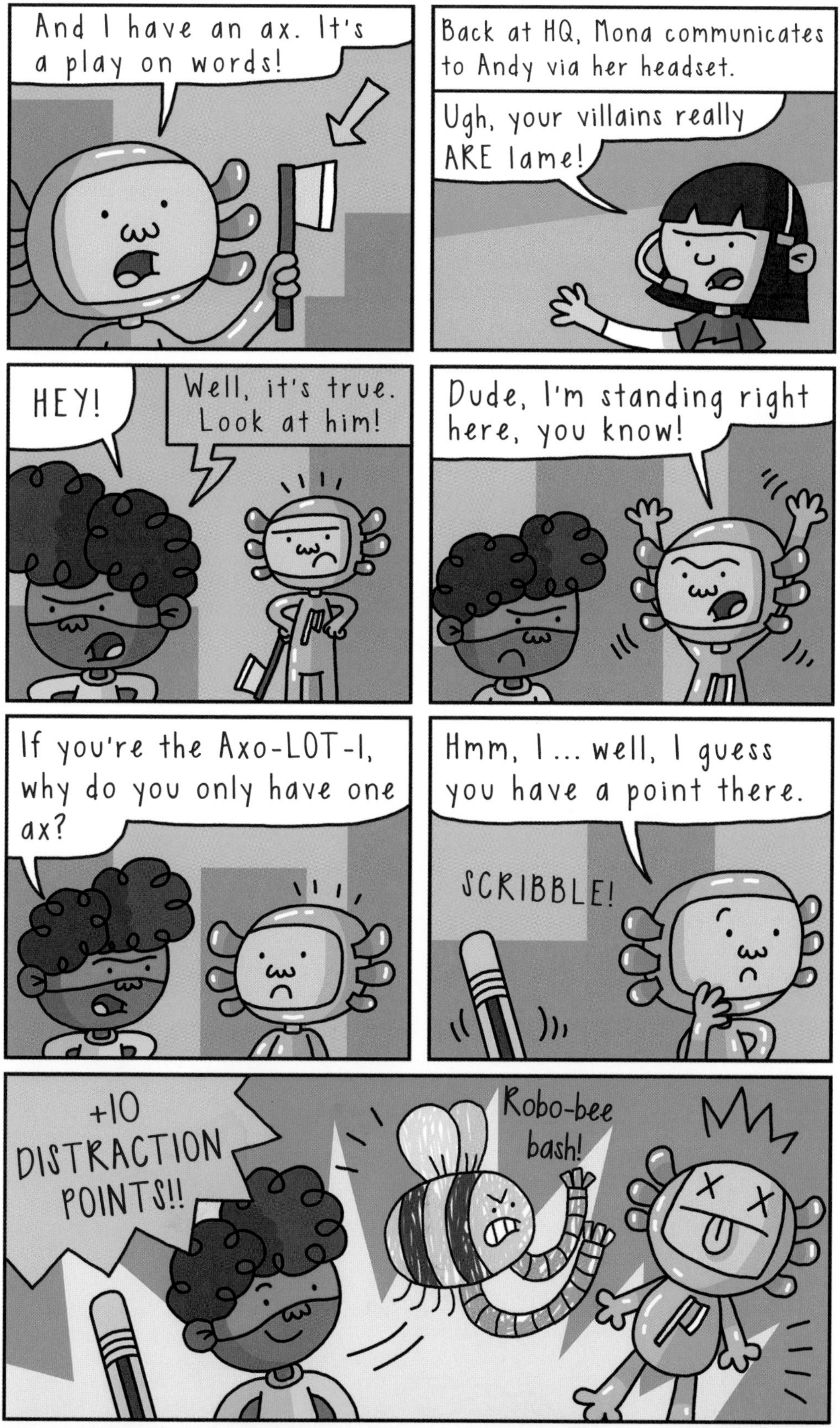

And I have an ax. It's a play on words!
Back at HQ, Mona communicates to Andy via her headset.
Ugh, your villains really ARE lame!
HEY!
Well, it's true. Look at him!
Dude, I'm standing right here, you know!
If you're the Axo-LOT-l, why do you only have one ax?
Hmm, I ... well, I guess you have a point there.
SCRIBBLE!
+10 DISTRACTION POINTS!!
Robo-bee bash!

Chapter 3 **Super Dweeb Fan Club**

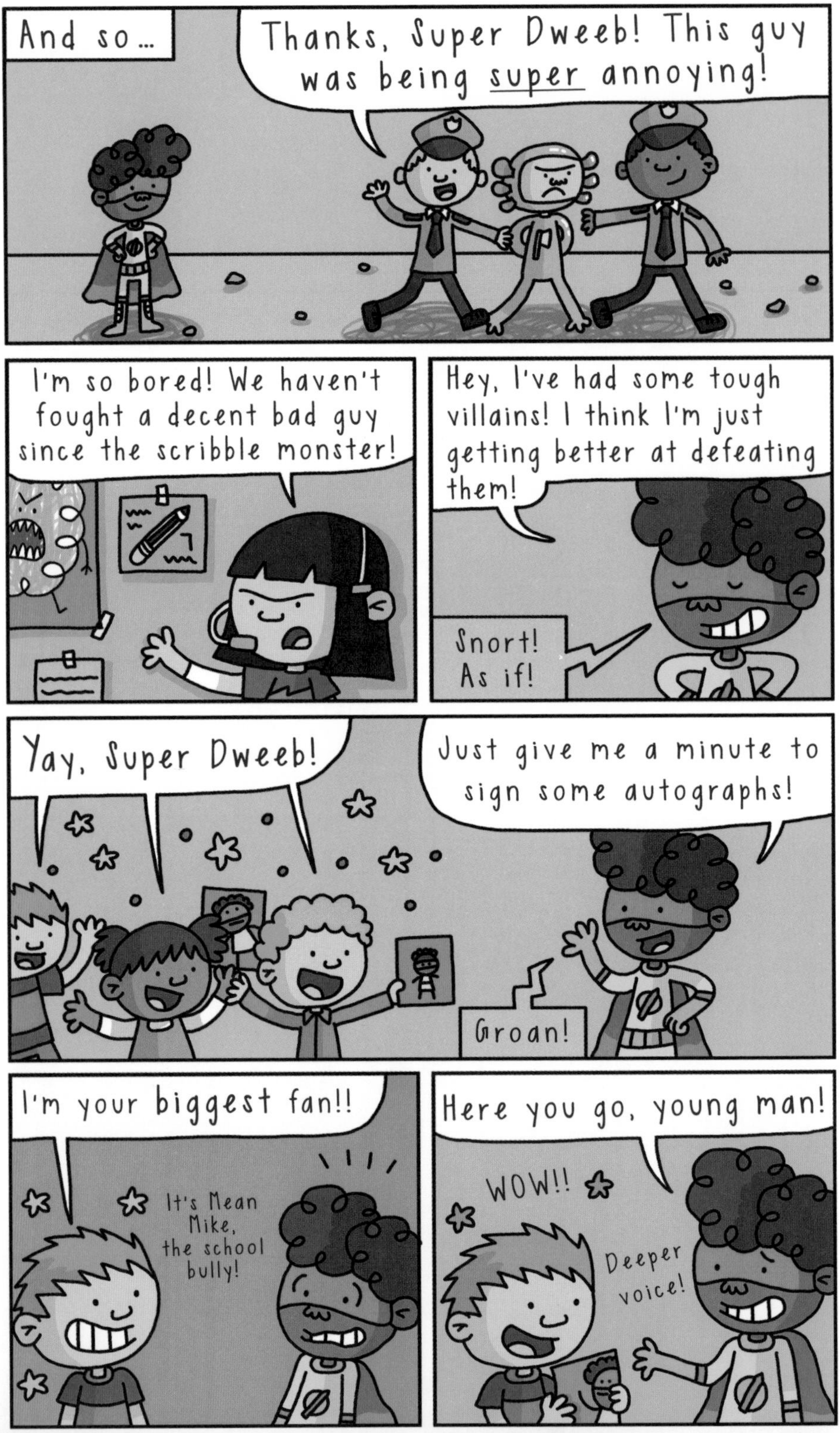
And so…
Thanks, Super Dweeb! This guy was being super annoying!
I'm so bored! We haven't fought a decent bad guy since the scribble monster!
Hey, I've had some tough villains! I think I'm just getting better at defeating them!
Snort! As if!
Yay, Super Dweeb!
Just give me a minute to sign some autographs!
Groan!
I'm your biggest fan!!
It's Mean Mike, the school bully!
Here you go, young man!
WOW!!
Deeper voice!

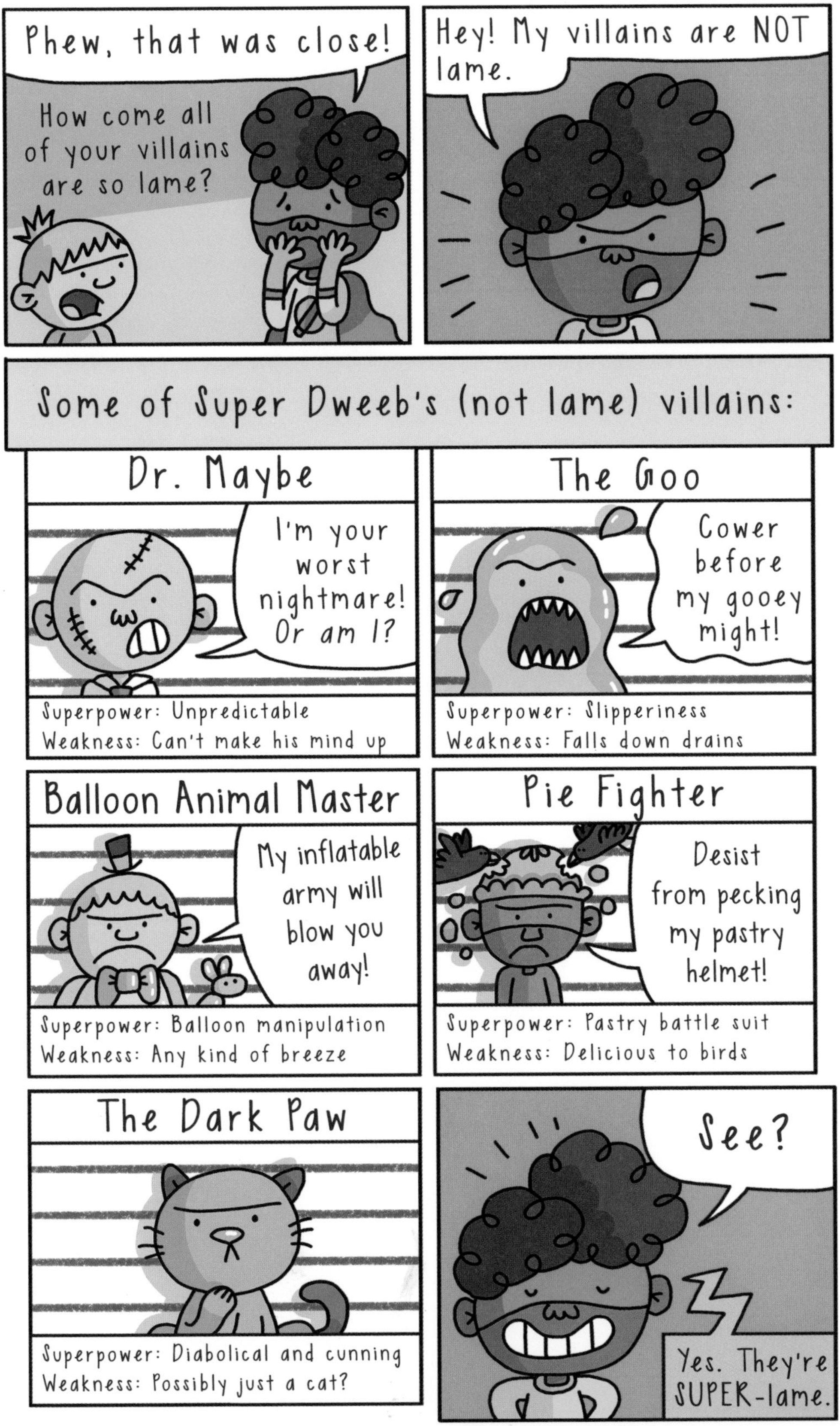

Phew, that was close!
How come all of your villains are so lame?
Hey! My villains are NOT lame.
Some of Super Dweeb's (not lame) villains:
Dr. Maybe
I'm your worst nightmare! Or am I?
Superpower: Unpredictable
Weakness: Can't make his mind up
The Goo
Cower before my gooey might!
Superpower: Slipperiness
Weakness: Falls down drains
Balloon Animal Master
My inflatable army will blow you away!
Superpower: Balloon manipulation
Weakness: Any kind of breeze
Pie Fighter
Desist from pecking my pastry helmet!
Superpower: Pastry battle suit
Weakness: Delicious to birds
The Dark Paw
Superpower: Diabolical and cunning
Weakness: Possibly just a cat?
See?
Yes. They're SUPER-lame.

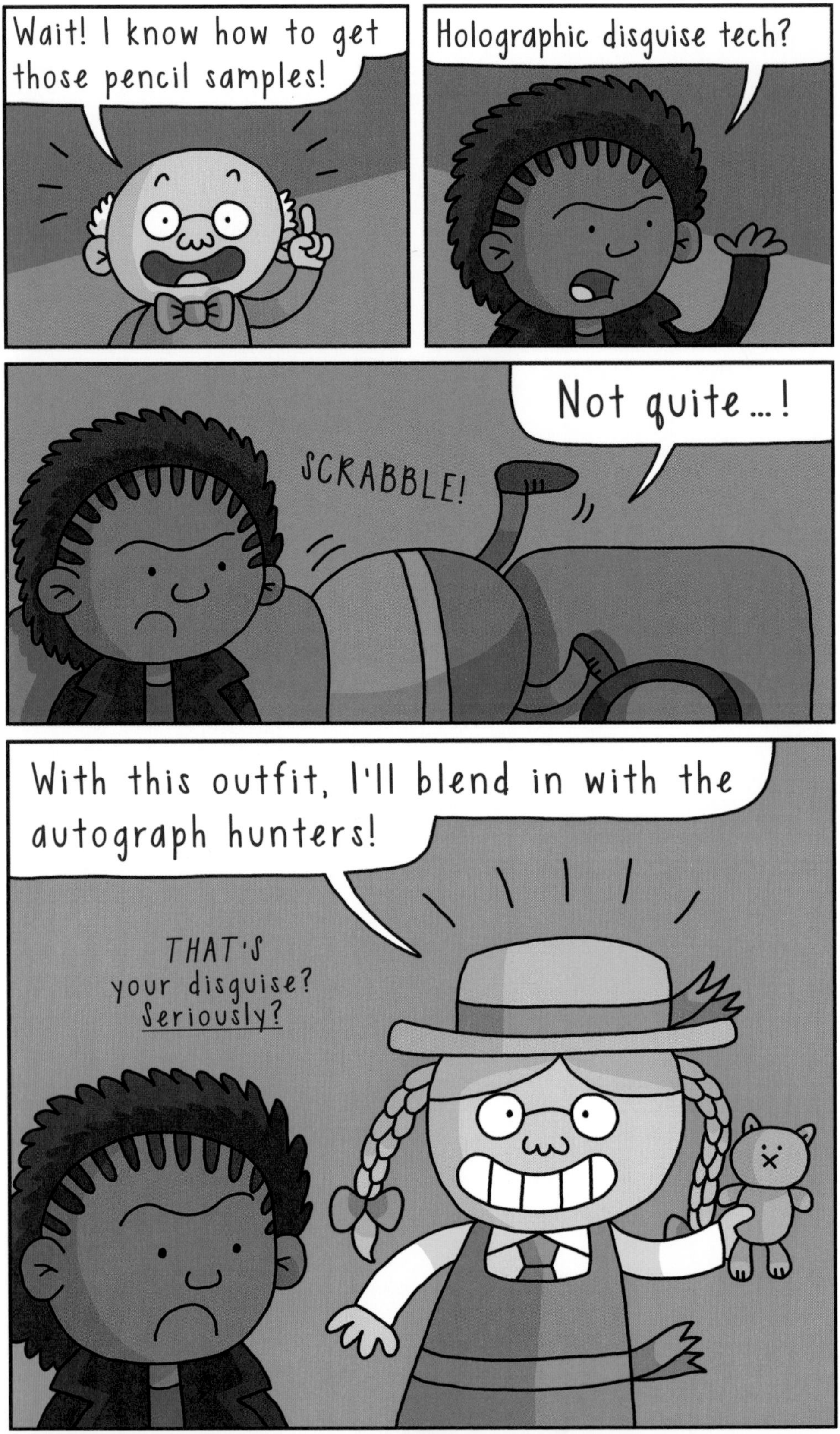
Wait! I know how to get those pencil samples!
Holographic disguise tech?
Not quite...!
SCRABBLE!
With this outfit, I'll blend in with the autograph hunters!
THAT'S your disguise? Seriously?

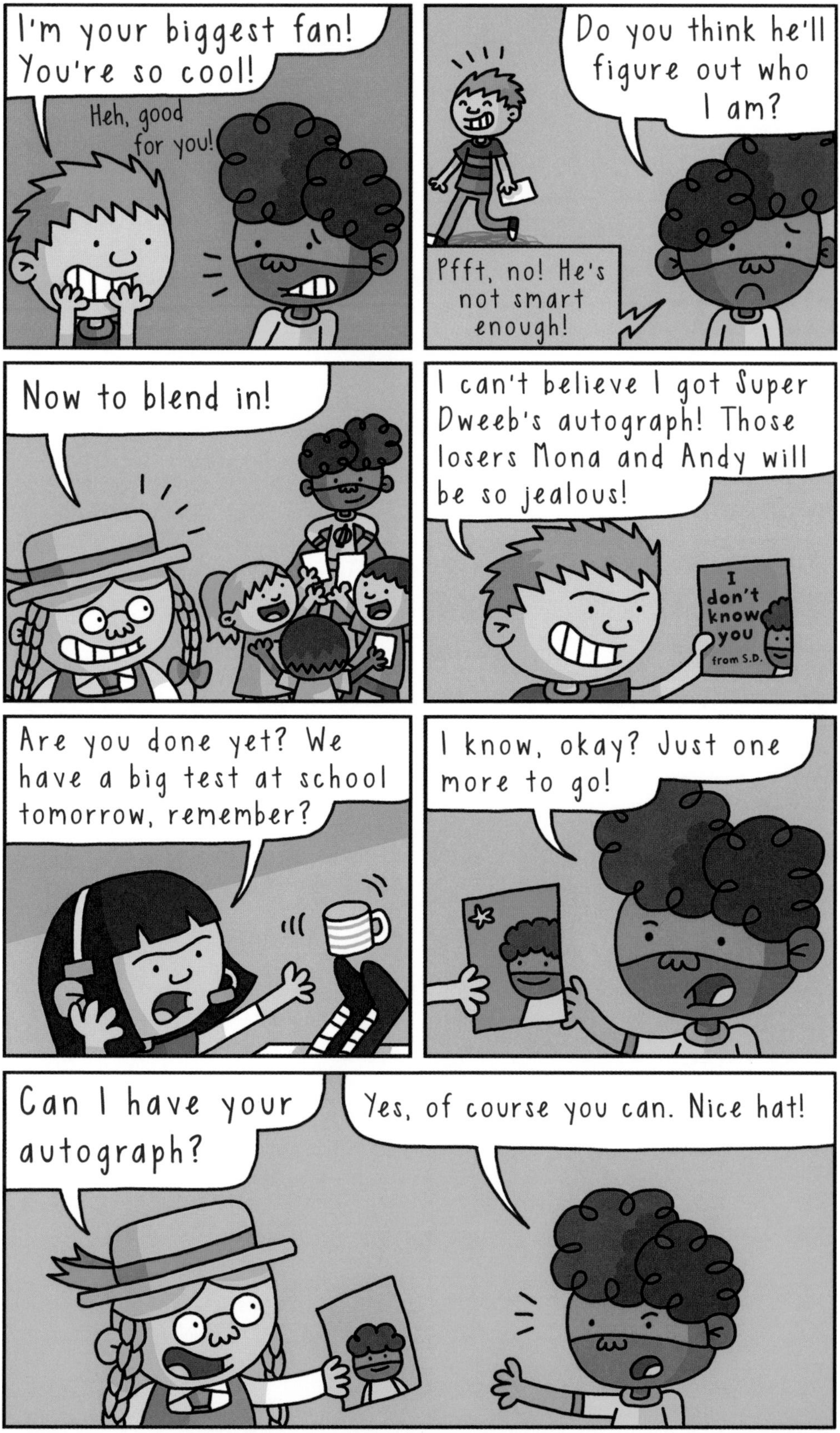
I'm your biggest fan! You're so cool!
Heh, good for you!
Do you think he'll figure out who I am?
Pfft, no! He's not smart enough!
Now to blend in!
I can't believe I got Super Dweeb's autograph! Those losers Mona and Andy will be so jealous!
I don't know you from S.D.
Are you done yet? We have a big test at school tomorrow, remember?
I know, okay? Just one more to go!
Can I have your autograph?
Yes, of course you can. Nice hat!

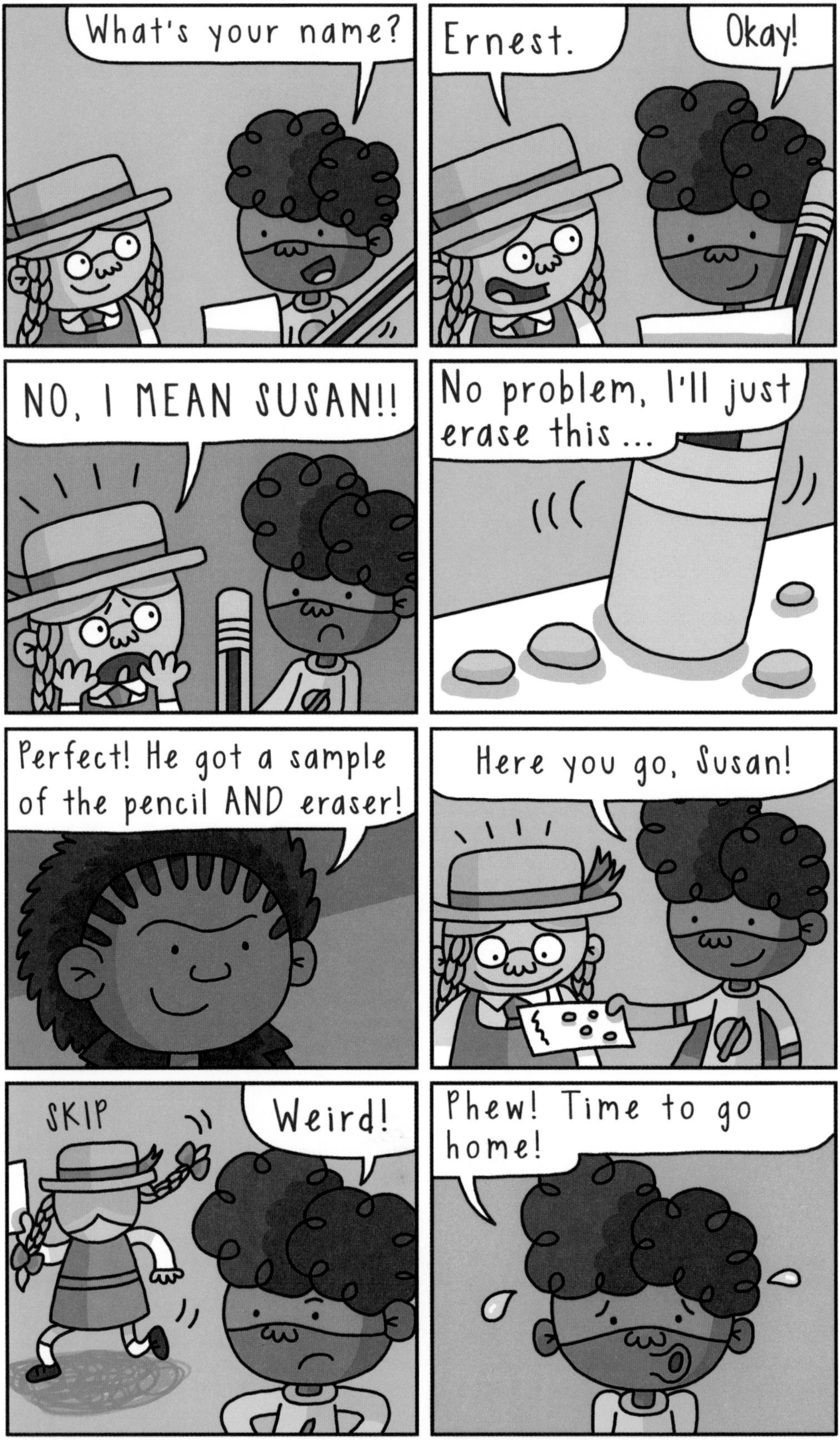
What's your name?
Ernest.
Okay!
NO, I MEAN SUSAN!!
No problem, I'll just erase this ...
Perfect! He got a sample of the pencil AND eraser!
Here you go, Susan!
SKIP
Weird!
Phew! Time to go home!

What a day! I was just about to go home and study when ...

SUPER DWEEB
MERCHANDISE FOR SALE!
Action figures!
Foam replica pencils!

NOOO! Oscar could blow everything!
It wouldn't take much for someone to
recognize him and realize that we're related!
I stormed over.

"OSCAR!" I hissed!

STOMP!

"WHAT ON EARTH ARE YOU DOING?"

I said.

"Being your manager!" Oscar said.

"THE FANS WANT MERCHANDISE
SO I MADE THIS ALL MYSELF!"

I tried not to get too angry.

"COME IN HERE, QUICK!"

I said between clenched teeth and dragged

Oscar into an alleyway.

Hey, my wagon!

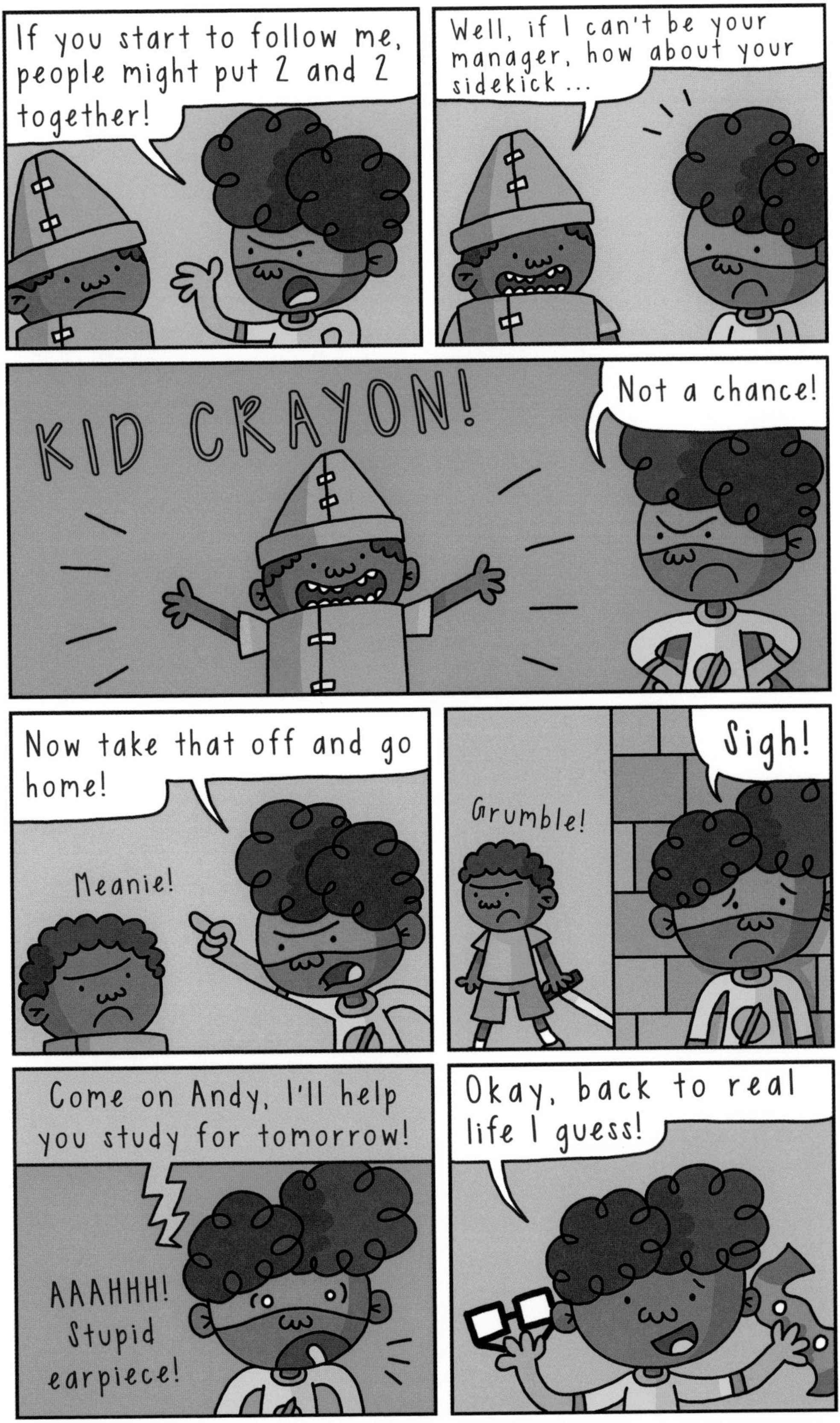
If you start to follow me, people might put 2 and 2 together!
Well, if I can't be your manager, how about your sidekick ...
KID CRAYON!
Not a chance!
Now take that off and go home!
Meanie!
Grumble!
Sigh!
Come on Andy, I'll help you study for tomorrow!
AAAHHH! Stupid earpiece!
Okay, back to real life I guess!

Chapter 4 **The Secret Origin of Doctor Eraser-Butt**

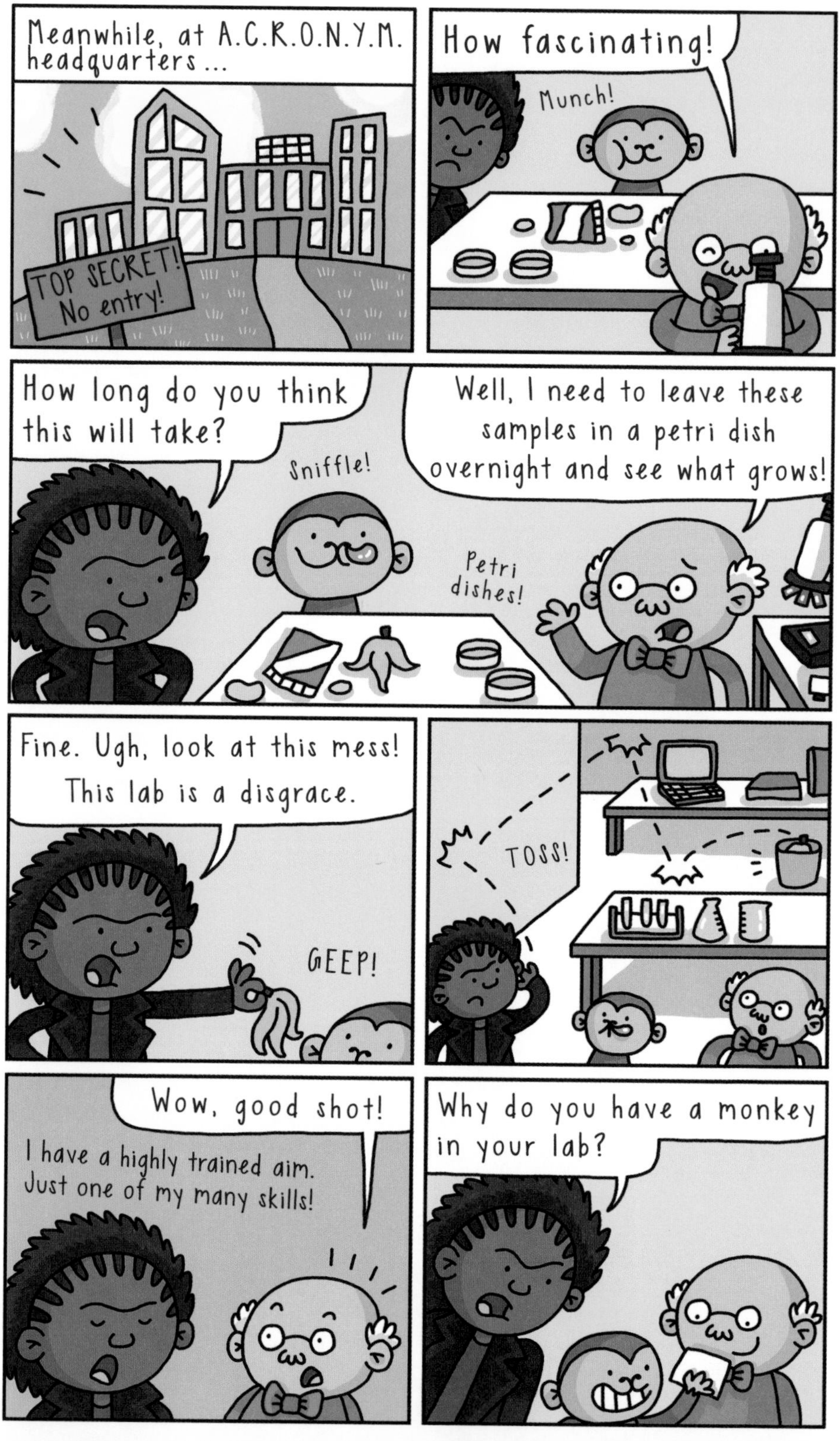
Meanwhile, at A.C.R.O.N.Y.M. headquarters ...
TOP SECRET! No entry!
How fascinating!
Munch!
How long do you think this will take?
Sniffle!
Well, I need to leave these samples in a petri dish overnight and see what grows!
Petri dishes!
Fine. Ugh, look at this mess! This lab is a disgrace.
GEEP!
TOSS!
Wow, good shot!
I have a highly trained aim. Just one of my many skills!
Why do you have a monkey in your lab?

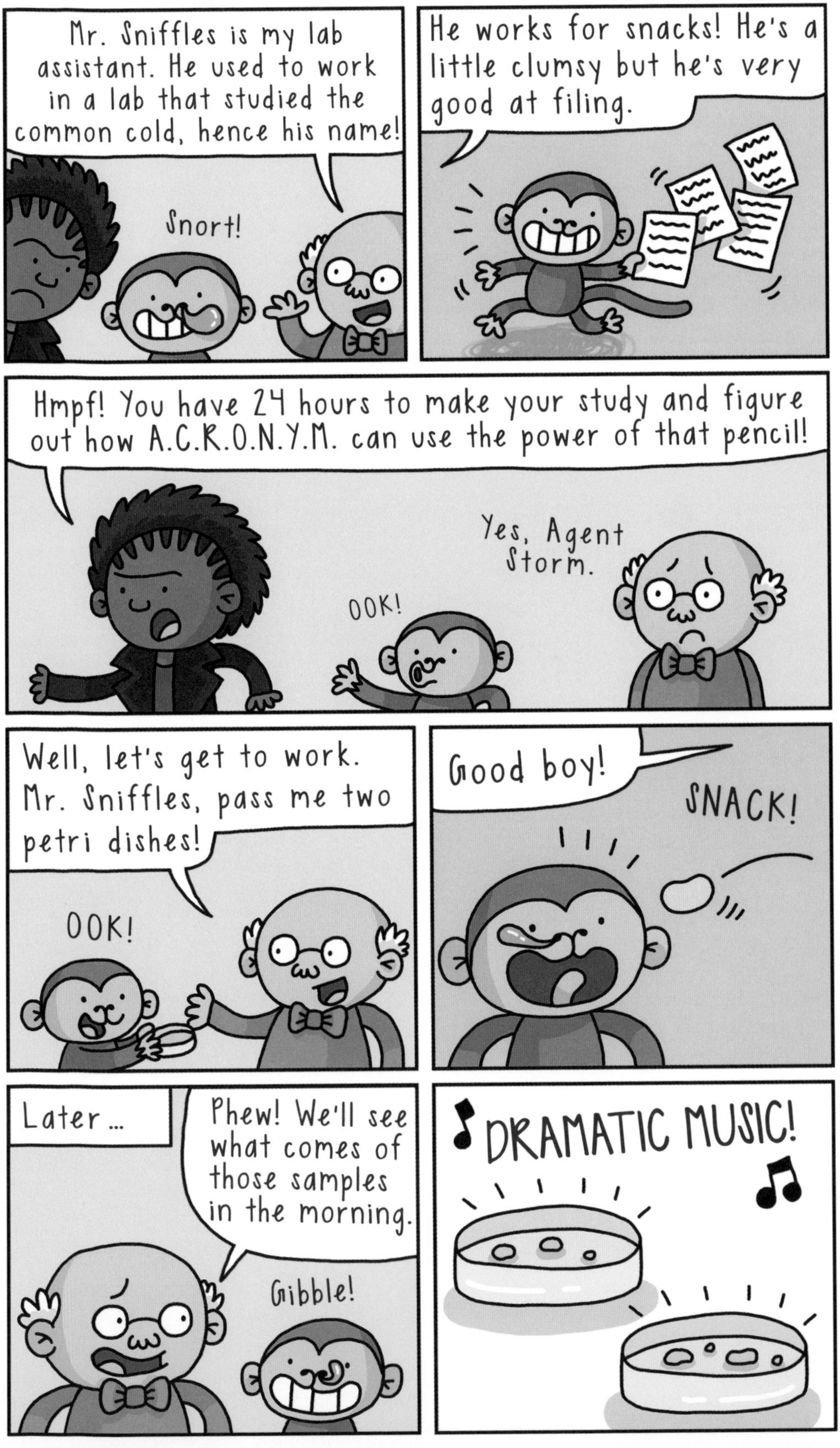

Mr. Sniffles is my lab assistant. He used to work in a lab that studied the common cold, hence his name!
Snort!
He works for snacks! He's a little clumsy but he's very good at filing.
Hmpf! You have 24 hours to make your study and figure out how A.C.R.O.N.Y.M. can use the power of that pencil!
Yes, Agent Storm.
OOK!
Well, let's get to work. Mr. Sniffles, pass me two petri dishes!
OOK!
Good boy!
SNACK!
Later ...
Phew! We'll see what comes of those samples in the morning.
Gibble!
DRAMATIC MUSIC!

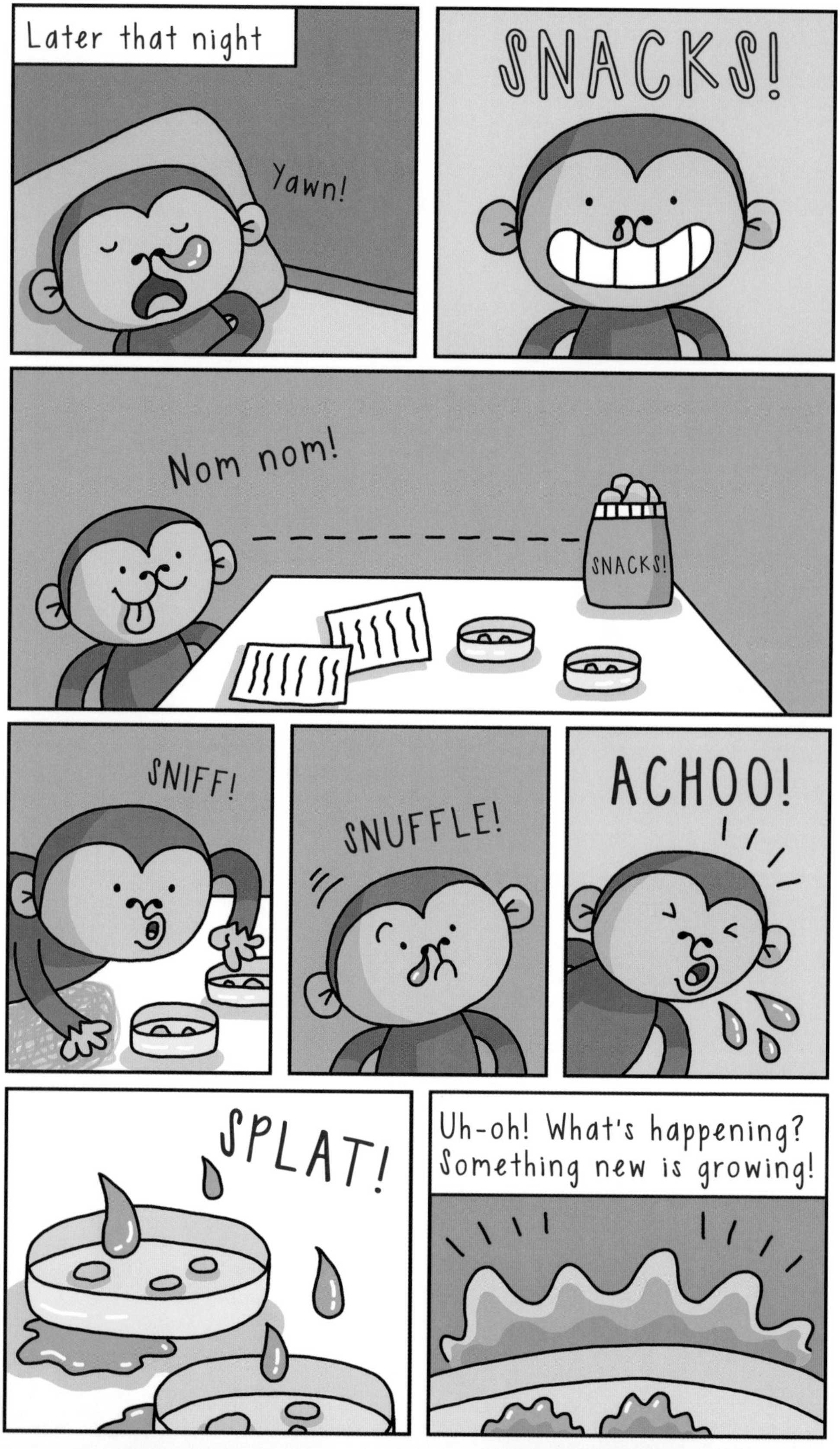
Later that night
Yawn!
SNACKS!
Nom nom!
SNACKS!
SNIFF!
SNUFFLE!
ACHOO!
SPLAT!
Uh-oh! What's happening?
Something new is growing!

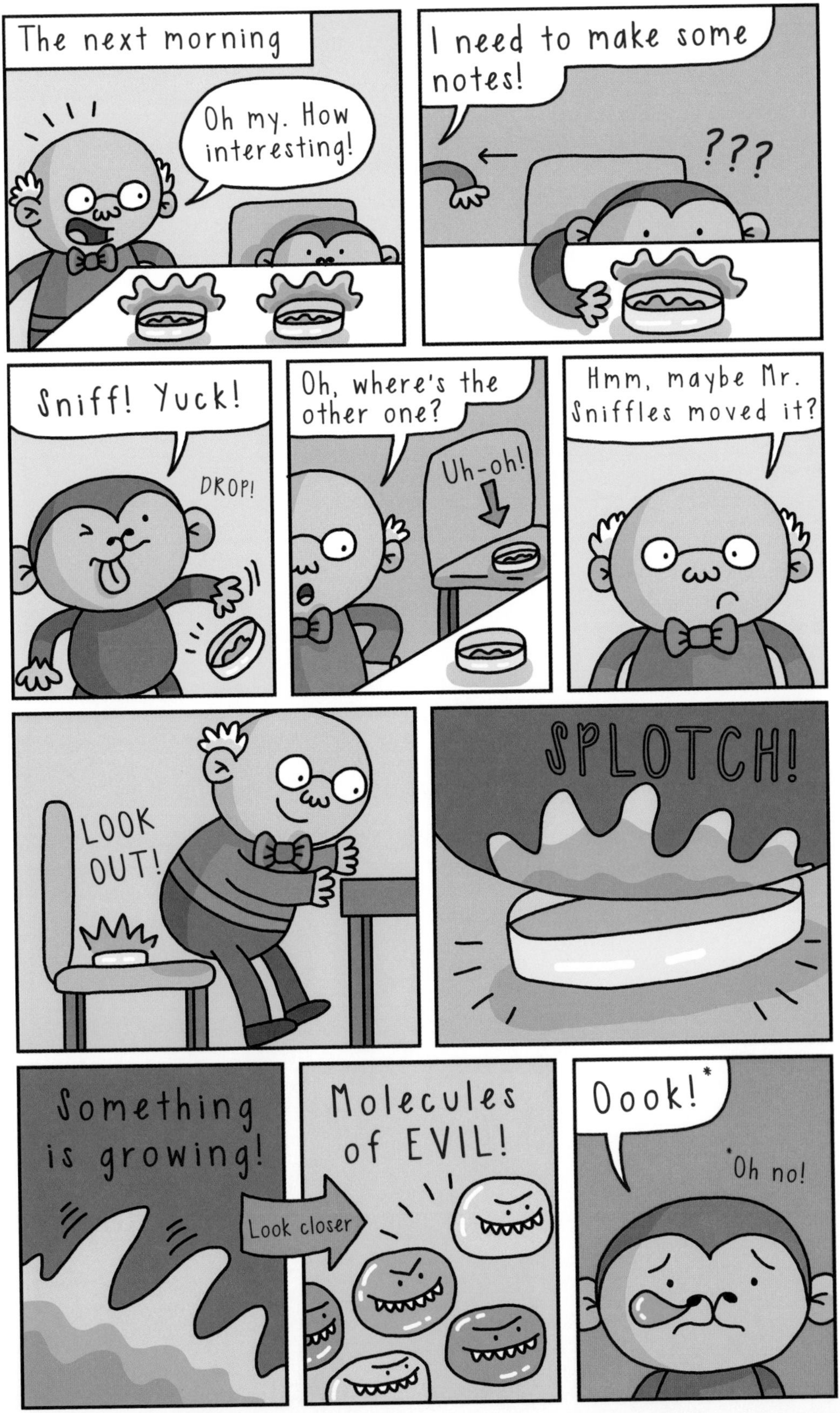
The next morning
Oh my. How interesting!
I need to make some notes!
???
Sniff! Yuck!
DROP!
Oh, where's the other one?
Uh-oh!
Hmm, maybe Mr. Sniffles moved it?
LOOK OUT!
SPLOTCH!
Something is growing!
Look closer
Molecules of EVIL!
Oook!*
*Oh no!

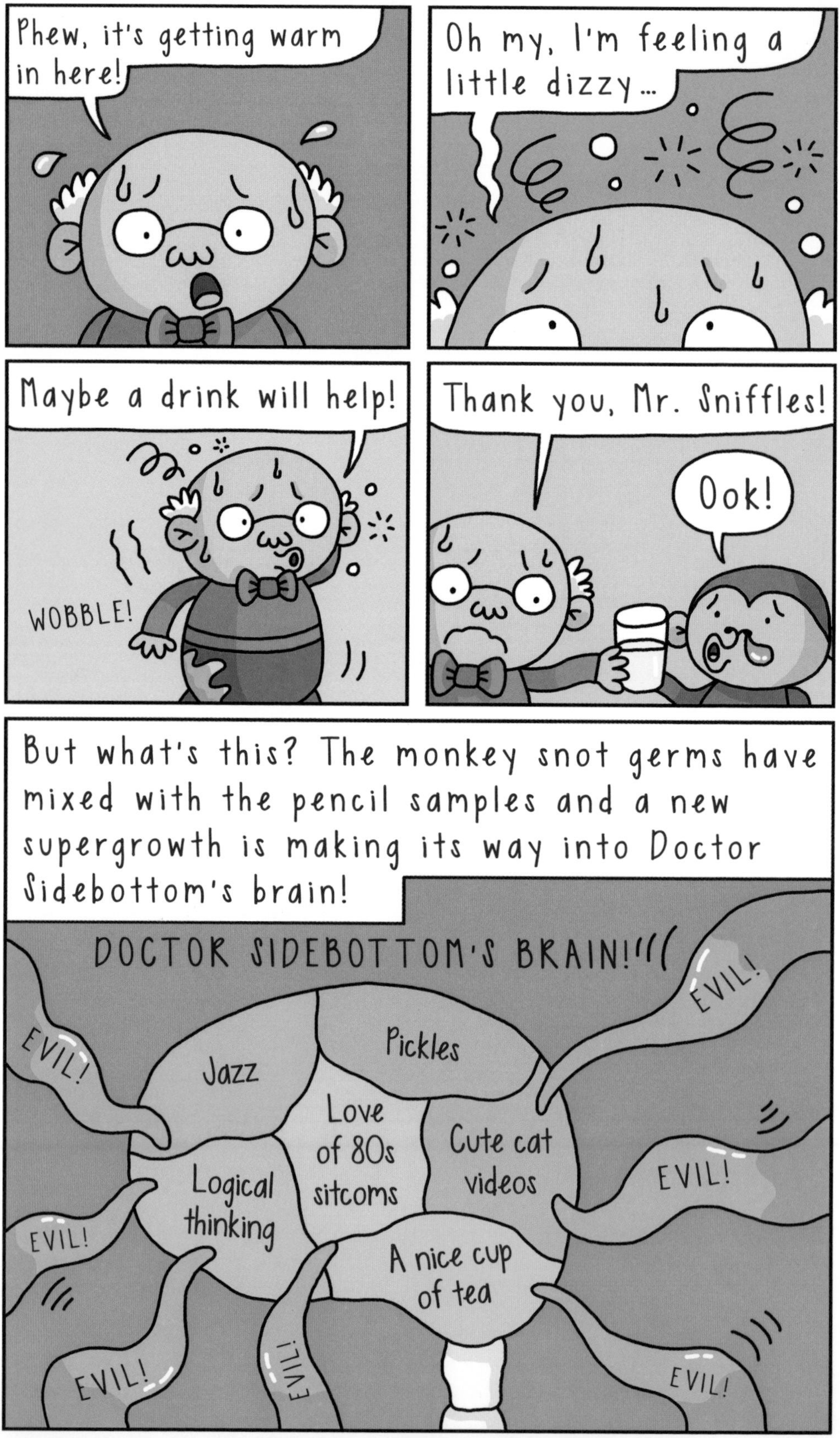
Phew, it's getting warm in here!
Oh my, I'm feeling a little dizzy...
Maybe a drink will help!
WOBBLE!
Thank you, Mr. Sniffles!
Ook!
But what's this? The monkey snot germs have mixed with the pencil samples and a new supergrowth is making its way into Doctor Sidebottom's brain!
DOCTOR SIDEBOTTOM'S BRAIN!
Jazz
Pickles
Love of 80s sitcoms
Cute cat videos
Logical thinking
A nice cup of tea
EVIL!
EVIL!
EVIL!
EVIL!
EVIL!
EVIL!
EVIL!

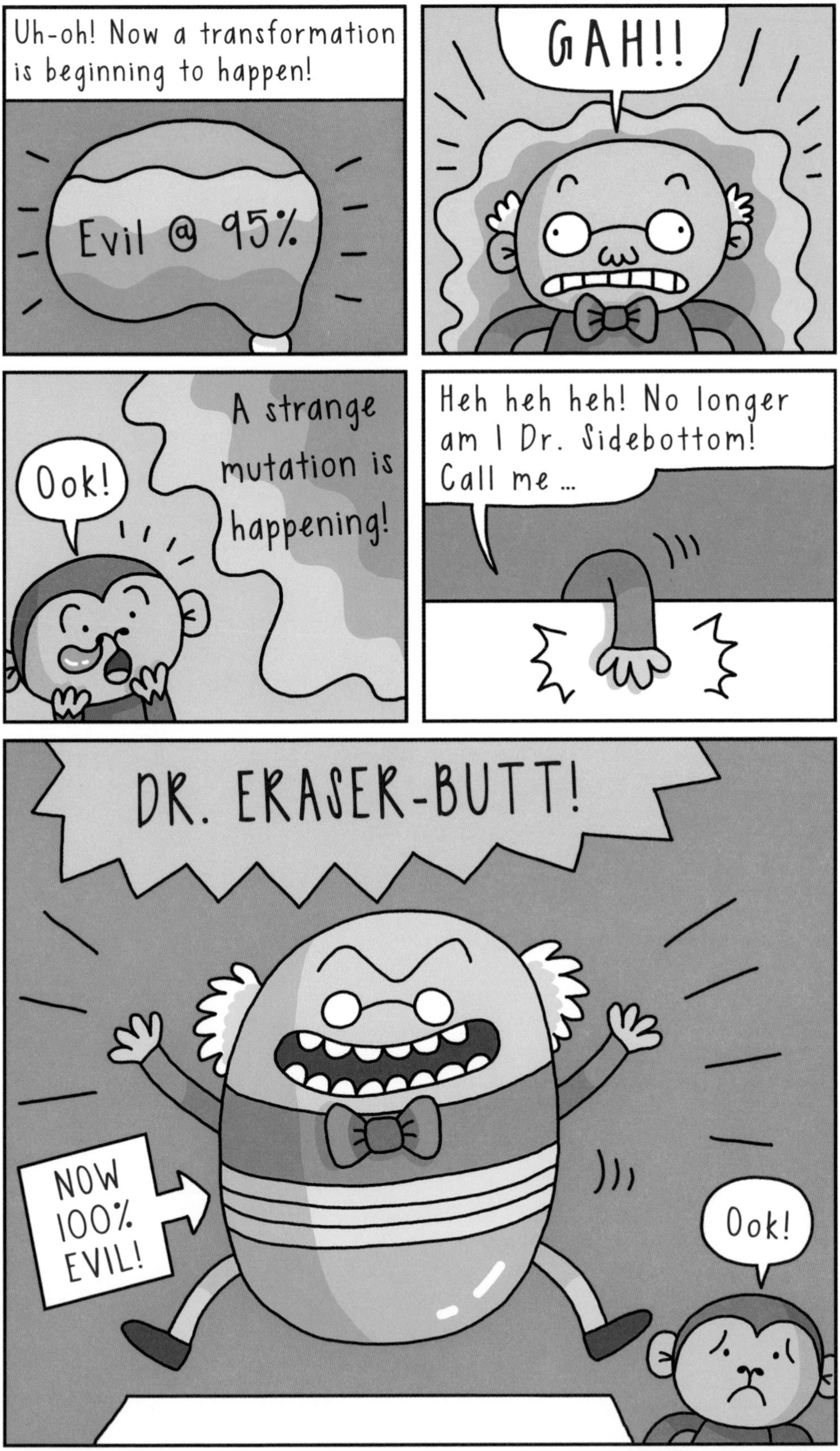

Uh-oh! Now a transformation is beginning to happen!
Evil @ 95%
GAH!!
A strange mutation is happening!
Ook!
Heh heh heh! No longer am I Dr. Sidebottom! Call me ...
DR. ERASER-BUTT!
NOW 100% EVIL!
Ook!

Chapter 5 **No Ifs, One Butt**

Back home ...

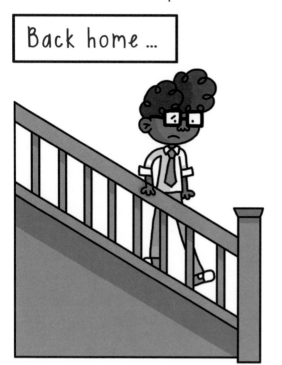

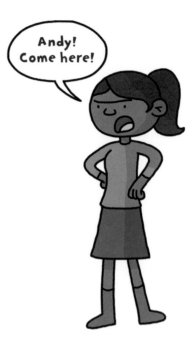

Andy! Come here!

I was truly in the doghouse!

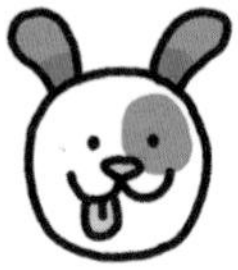

Wuf! (Sorry, Taters! Not that kind!)

"I've got you a tutor," said Mom. "You can go to the library to study but then come straight home, no ifs or buts!"

"But I don't need a tutor!" I said. I stopped complaining when Mom threatened her death glare.

"Who's the tutor?" I asked.

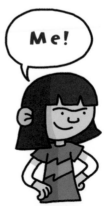

Me!
AHHH!

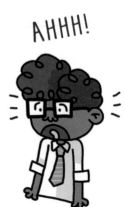

"Mona is going to make sure you study instead of doodling your silly comic books," said Mom.

"I think you mean *EPIC* comic books!" I exclaimed.

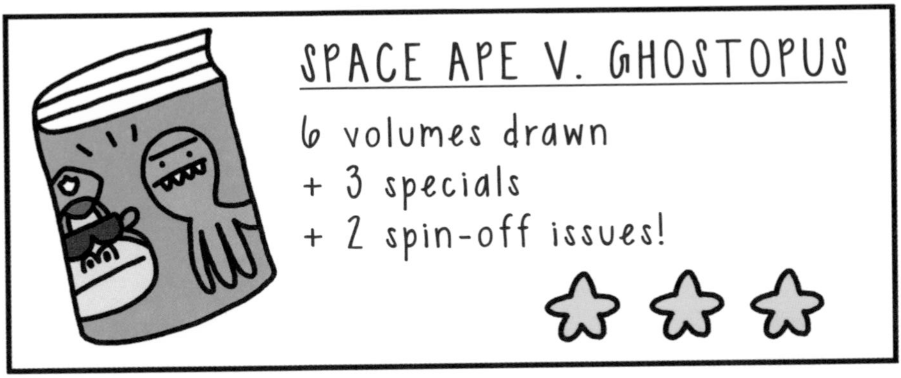
SPACE APE V. GHOSTOPUS
6 volumes drawn
+ 3 specials
+ 2 spin-off issues!

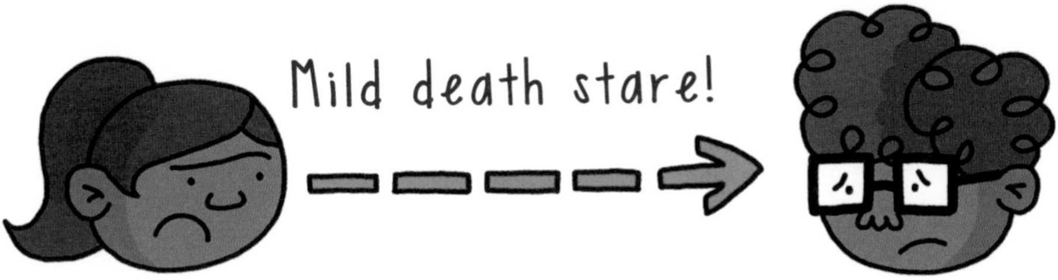
Mild death stare!

"Pass that test and you won't be grounded!"

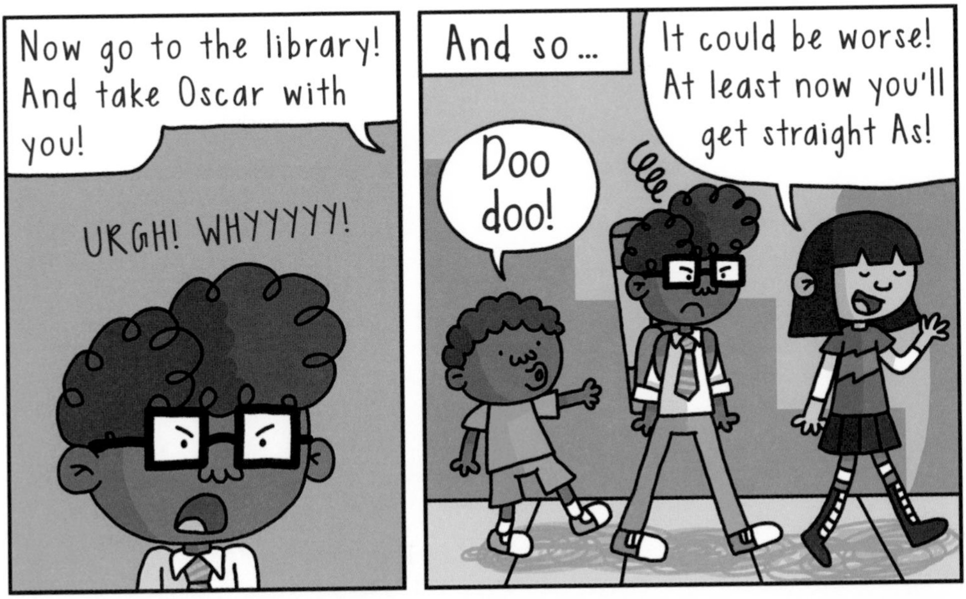
Now go to the library! And take Oscar with you!
URGH! WHYYYYY!
And so...
It could be worse! At least now you'll get straight As!
Doo doo!

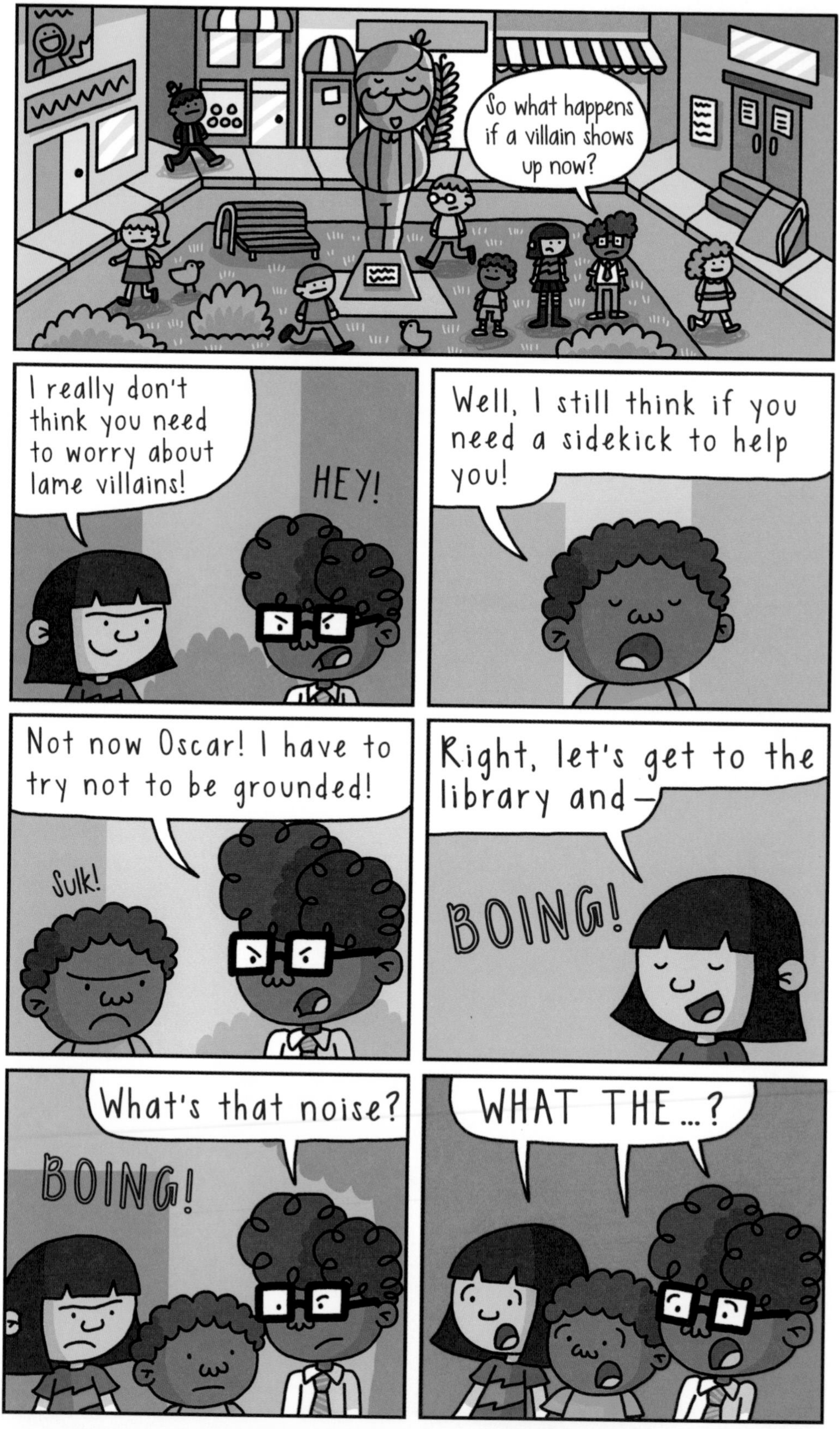
So what happens if a villain shows up now?
I really don't think you need to worry about lame villains!
HEY!
Well, I still think if you need a sidekick to help you!
Not now Oscar! I have to try not to be grounded!
Sulk!
Right, let's get to the library and–
BOING!
What's that noise?
BOING!
WHAT THE...?

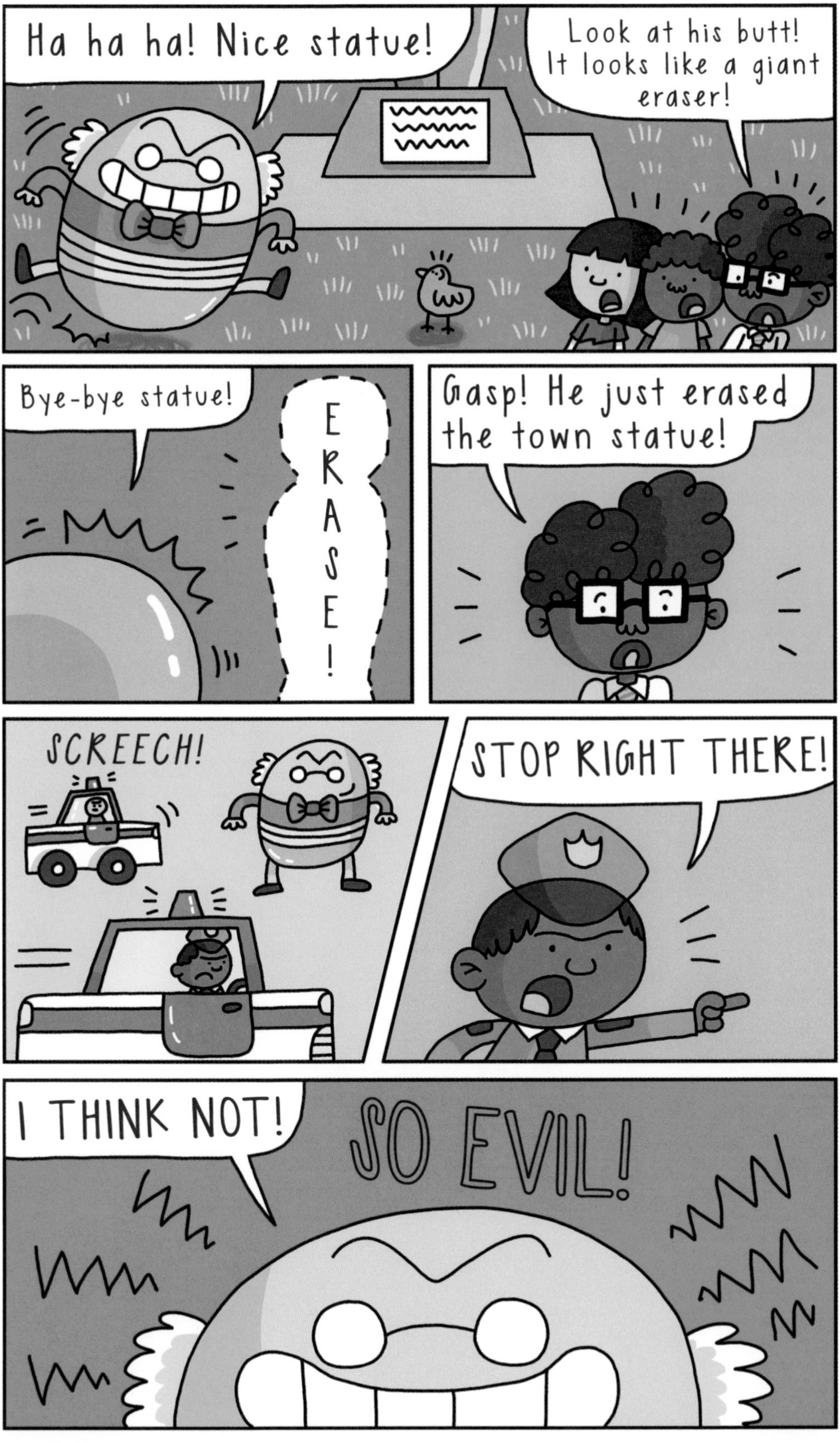

Ha ha ha! Nice statue!
Look at his butt! It looks like a giant eraser!
Bye-bye statue!
ERASE!
Gasp! He just erased the town statue!
SCREECH!
STOP RIGHT THERE!
I THINK NOT!
SO EVIL!

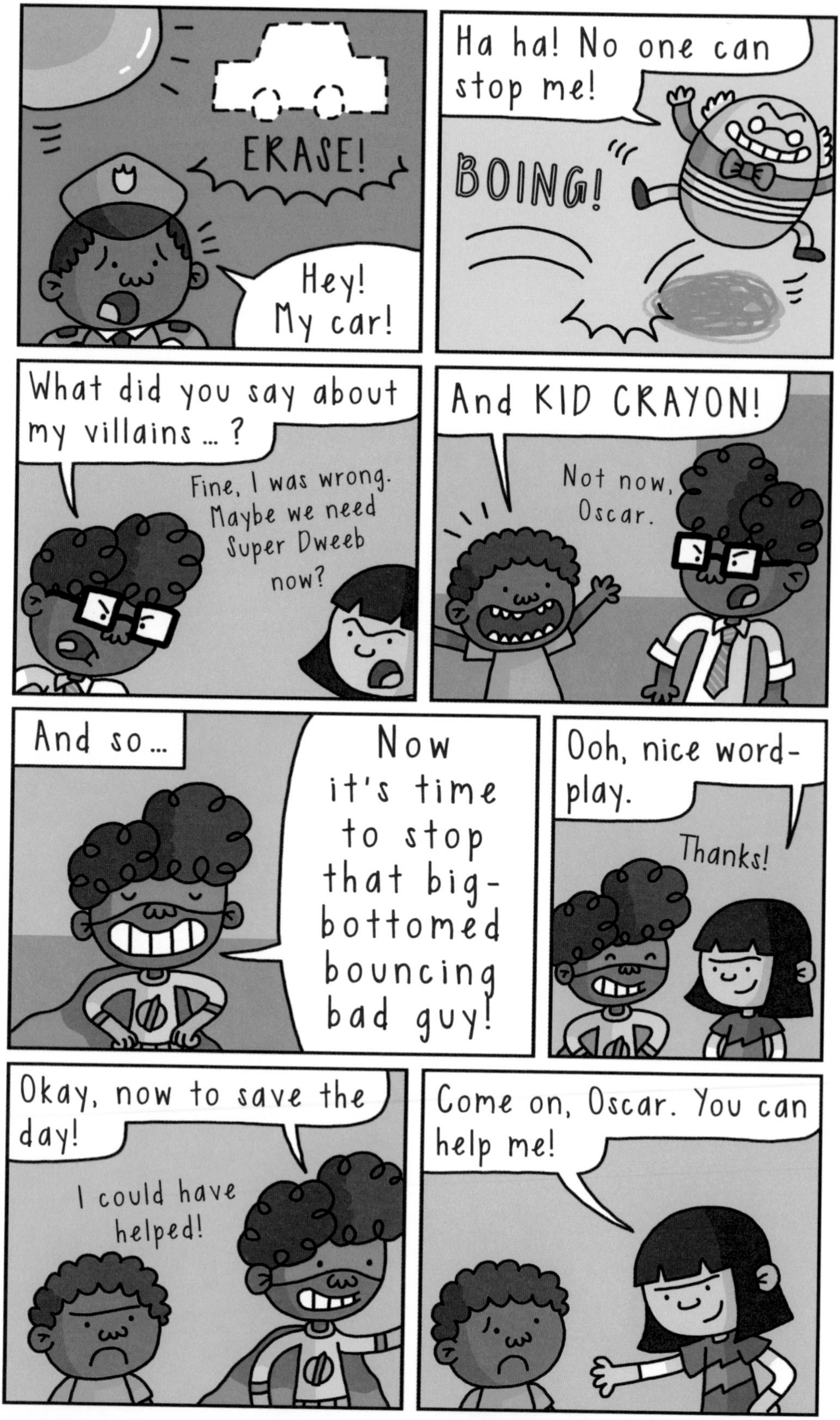
ERASE!
Hey! My car!
Ha ha! No one can stop me!
BOING!
What did you say about my villains ... ?
Fine, I was wrong. Maybe we need Super Dweeb now?
And KID CRAYON!
Not now, Oscar.
And so ...
Now it's time to stop that big-bottomed bouncing bad guy!
Ooh, nice word-play.
Thanks!
Okay, now to save the day!
I could have helped!
Come on, Oscar. You can help me!

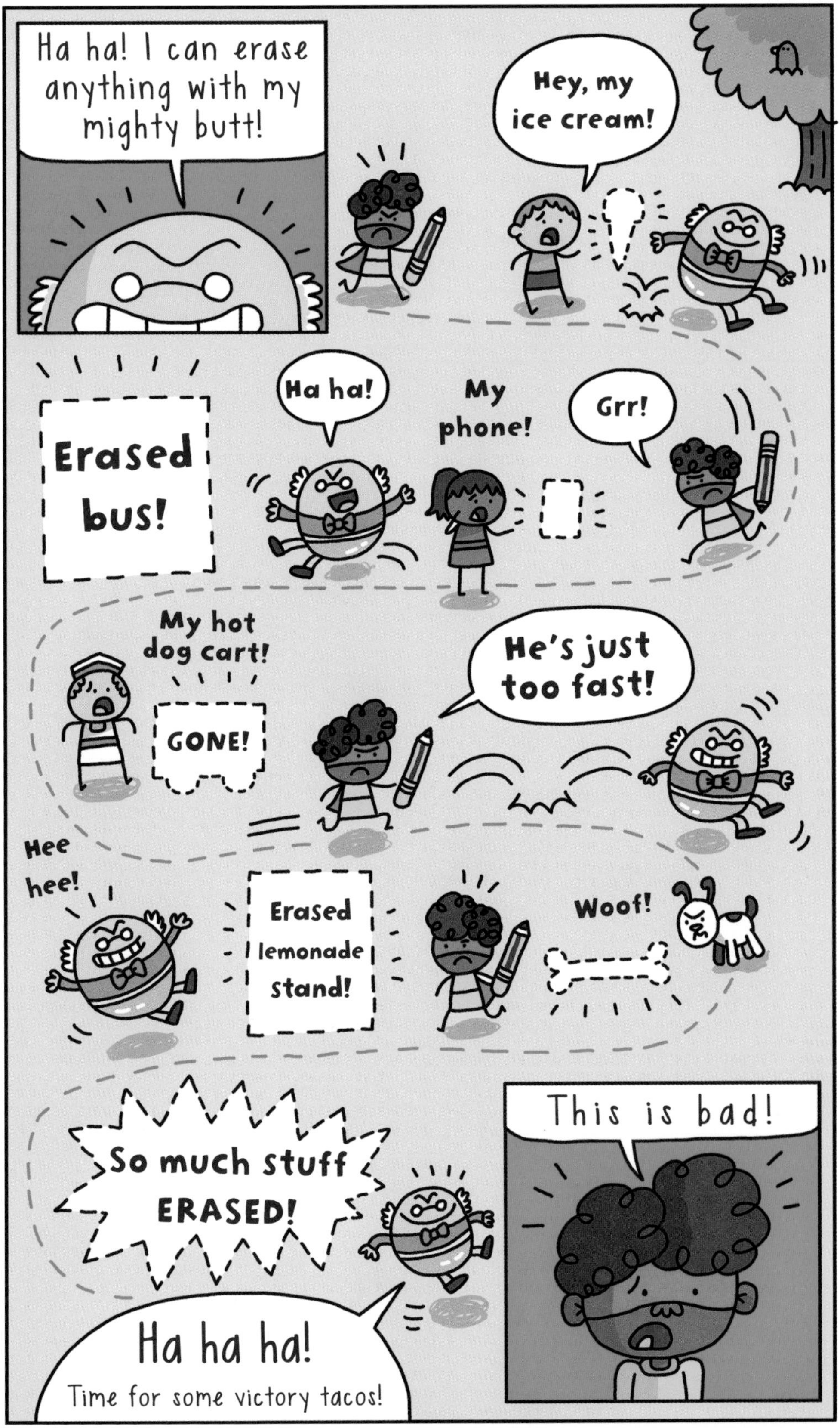

Ha ha! I can erase anything with my mighty butt!
Hey, my ice cream!
Erased bus!
Ha ha!
My phone!
Grr!
My hot dog cart!
GONE!
He's just too fast!
Hee hee!
Erased lemonade stand!
Woof!
So much stuff ERASED!
This is bad!
Ha ha ha!
Time for some victory tacos!

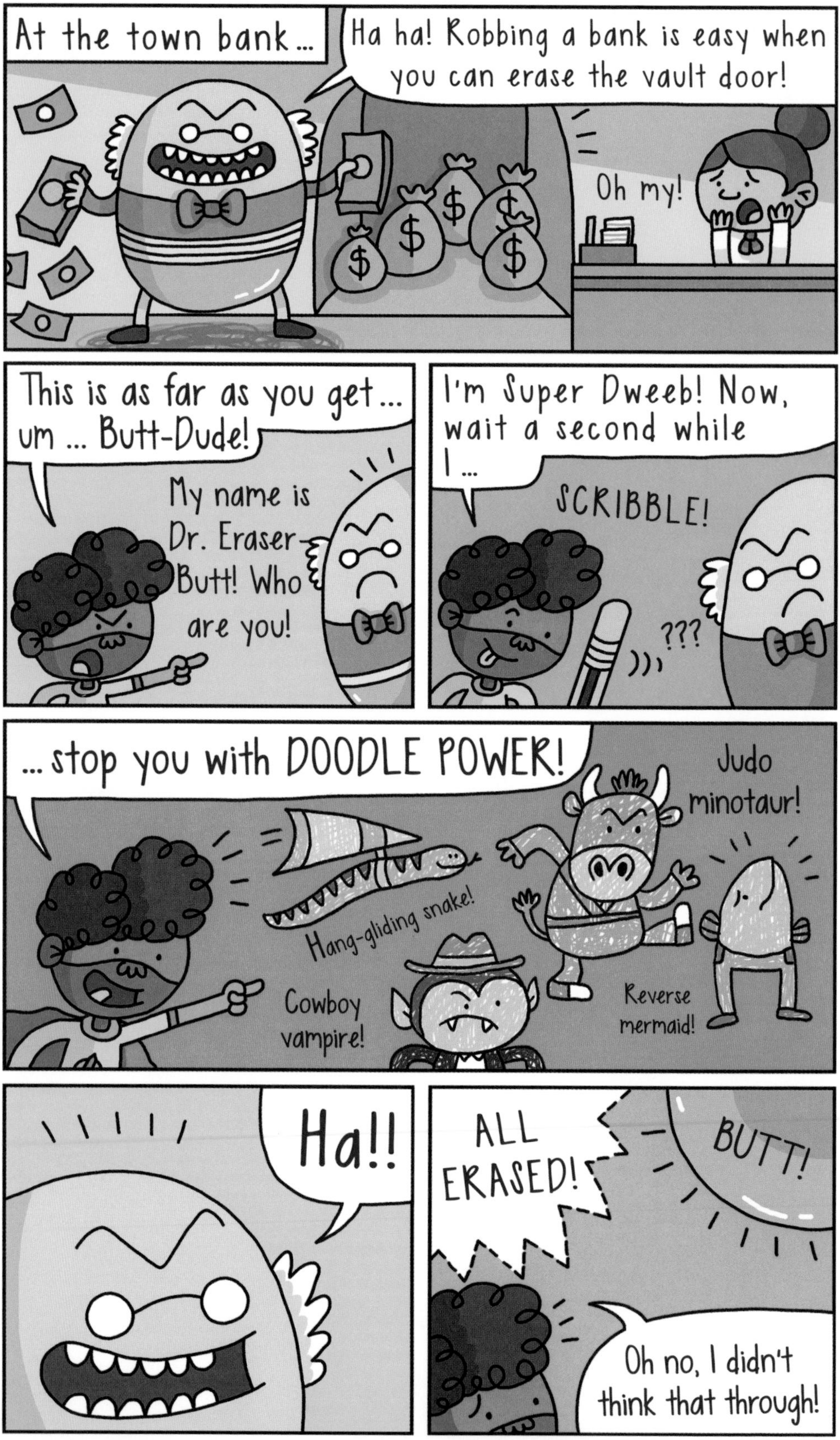
At the town bank ...
Ha ha! Robbing a bank is easy when you can erase the vault door!
Oh my!
This is as far as you get ... um ... Butt-Dude!
My name is Dr. Eraser-Butt! Who are you!
I'm Super Dweeb! Now, wait a second while I ...
SCRIBBLE!
???
... stop you with DOODLE POWER!
Judo minotaur!
Hang-gliding snake!
Cowboy vampire!
Reverse mermaid!
Ha!!
ALL ERASED!
BUTT!
Oh no, I didn't think that through!

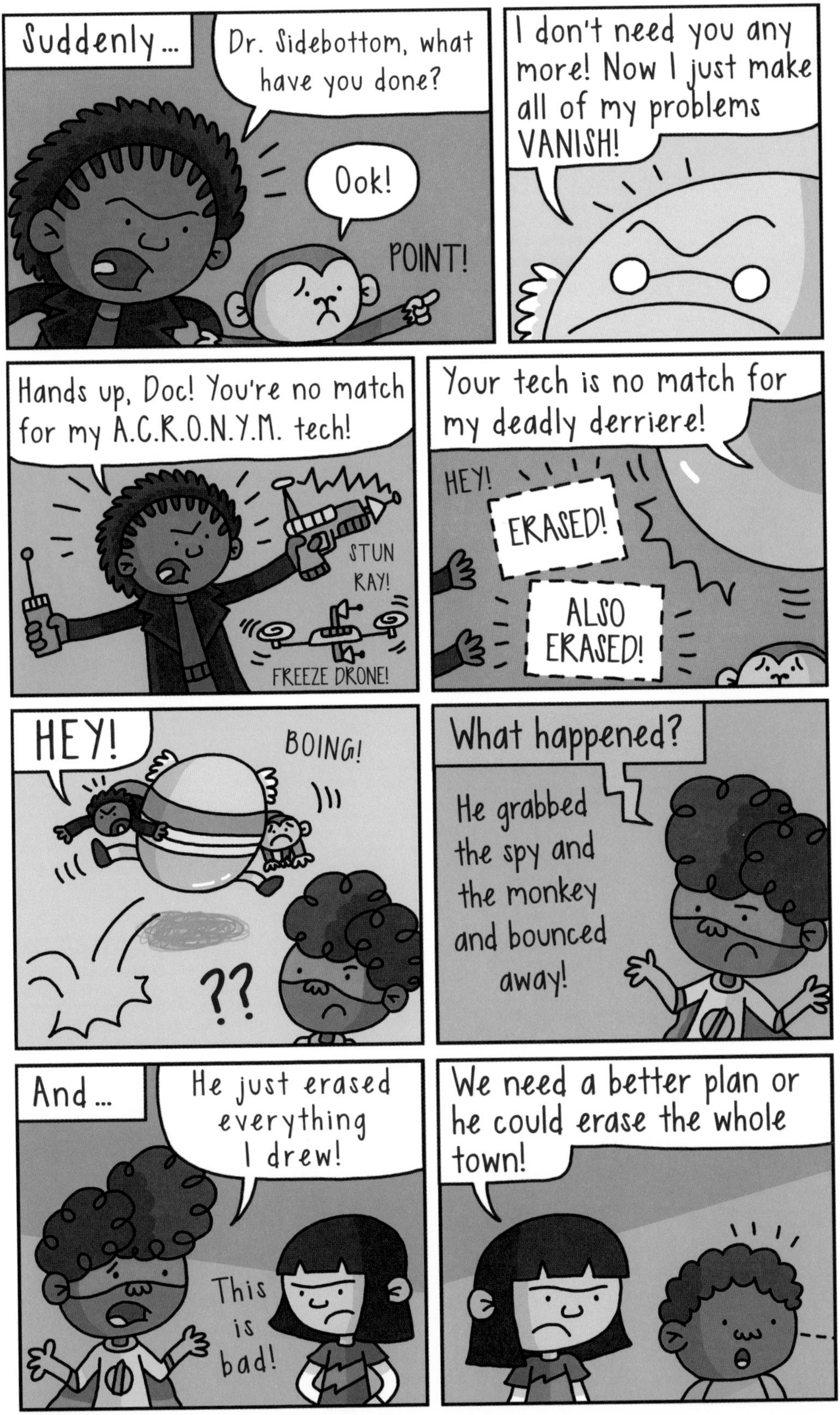
Suddenly ...
Dr. Sidebottom, what have you done?
Ook!
POINT!
I don't need you any more! Now I just make all of my problems VANISH!
Hands up, Doc! You're no match for my A.C.R.O.N.Y.M. tech!
STUN RAY!
FREEZE DRONE!
Your tech is no match for my deadly derriere!
HEY!
ERASED!
ALSO ERASED!
HEY!
BOING!
??
What happened?
He grabbed the spy and the monkey and bounced away!
And ...
He just erased everything I drew!
This is bad!
We need a better plan or he could erase the whole town!

Chapter 6 Kid Crayon Investigates

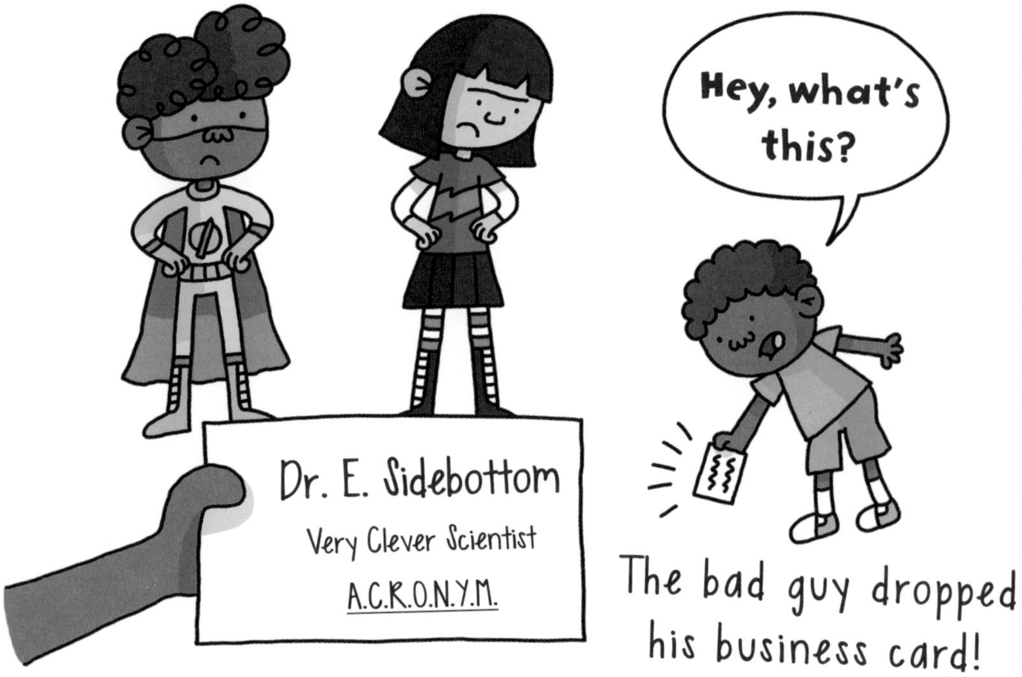
Hey, what's this?
Dr. E. Sidebottom
Very Clever Scientist
A.C.R.O.N.Y.M.
The bad guy dropped his business card!

"Okay, we have a lead," said Mona. "I guess a villain who drops his business card can't be all that competent."

"So what now?" I asked.

"We hit the computer and find out what A.C.R.O.N.Y.M. means!" said Mona.

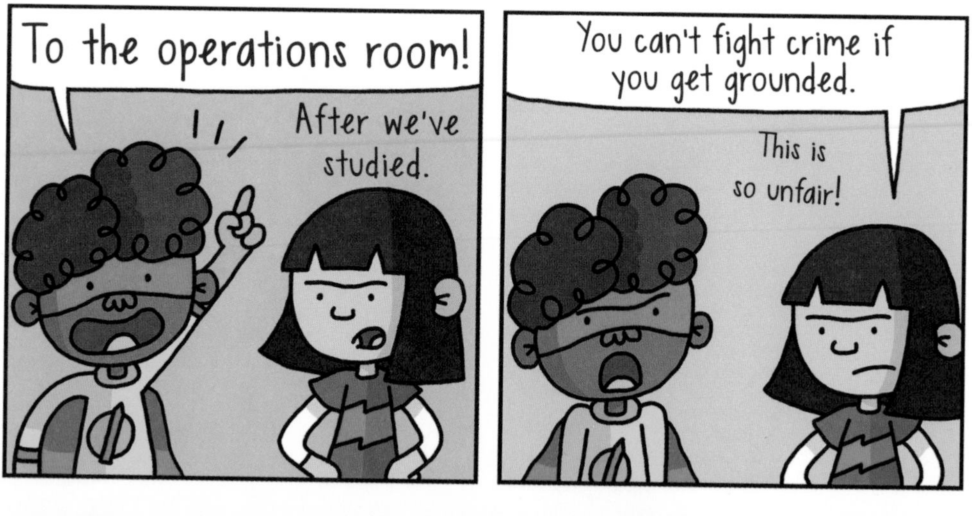
To the operations room!
After we've studied.
You can't fight crime if you get grounded.
This is so unfair!

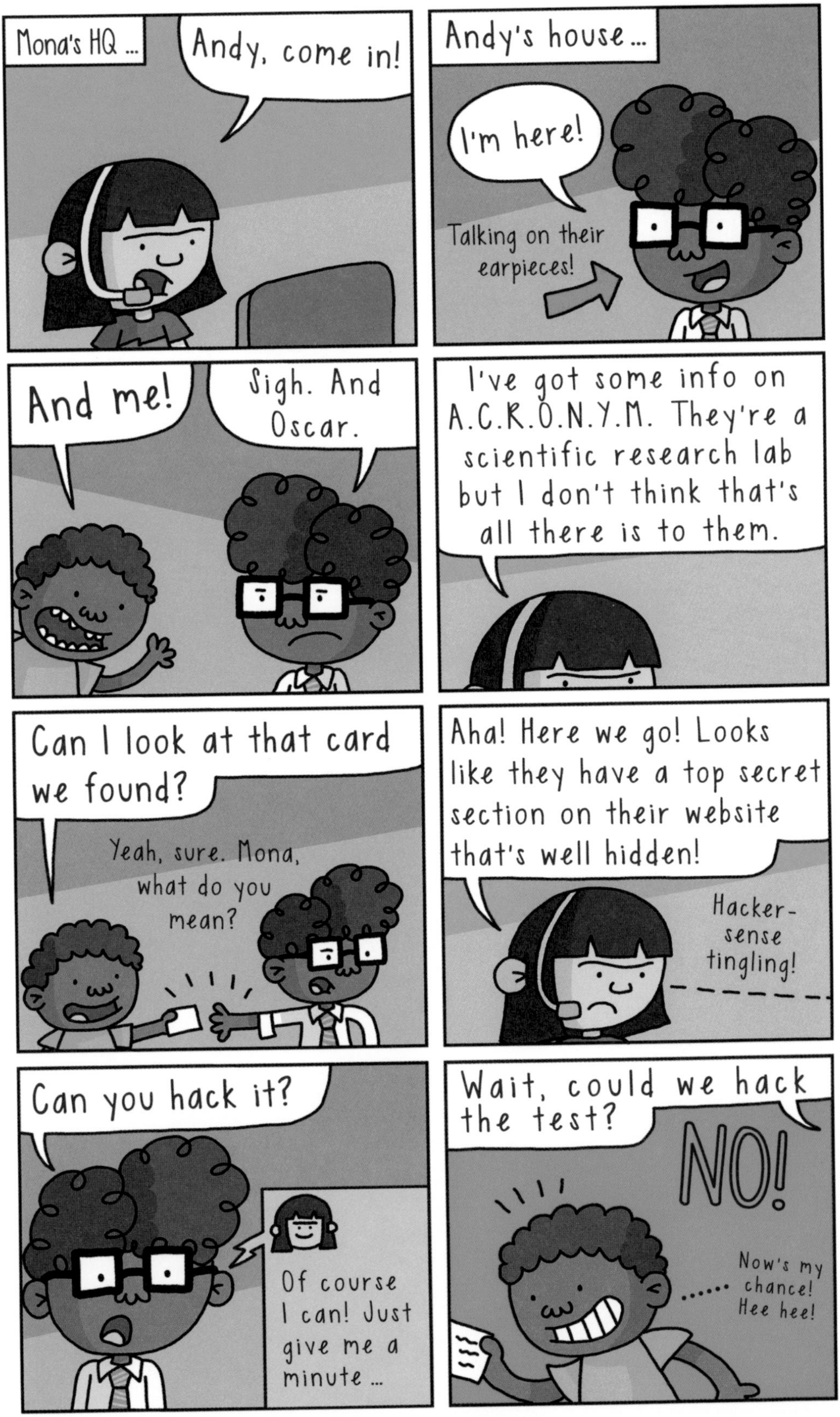
Mona's HQ ...
Andy, come in!
Andy's house ...
I'm here!
Talking on their earpieces!
And me!
Sigh. And Oscar.
I've got some info on A.C.R.O.N.Y.M. They're a scientific research lab but I don't think that's all there is to them.
Can I look at that card we found?
Yeah, sure. Mona, what do you mean?
Aha! Here we go! Looks like they have a top secret section on their website that's well hidden!
Hacker-sense tingling!
Can you hack it?
Of course I can! Just give me a minute ...
Wait, could we hack the test?
NO!
Now's my chance! Hee hee!

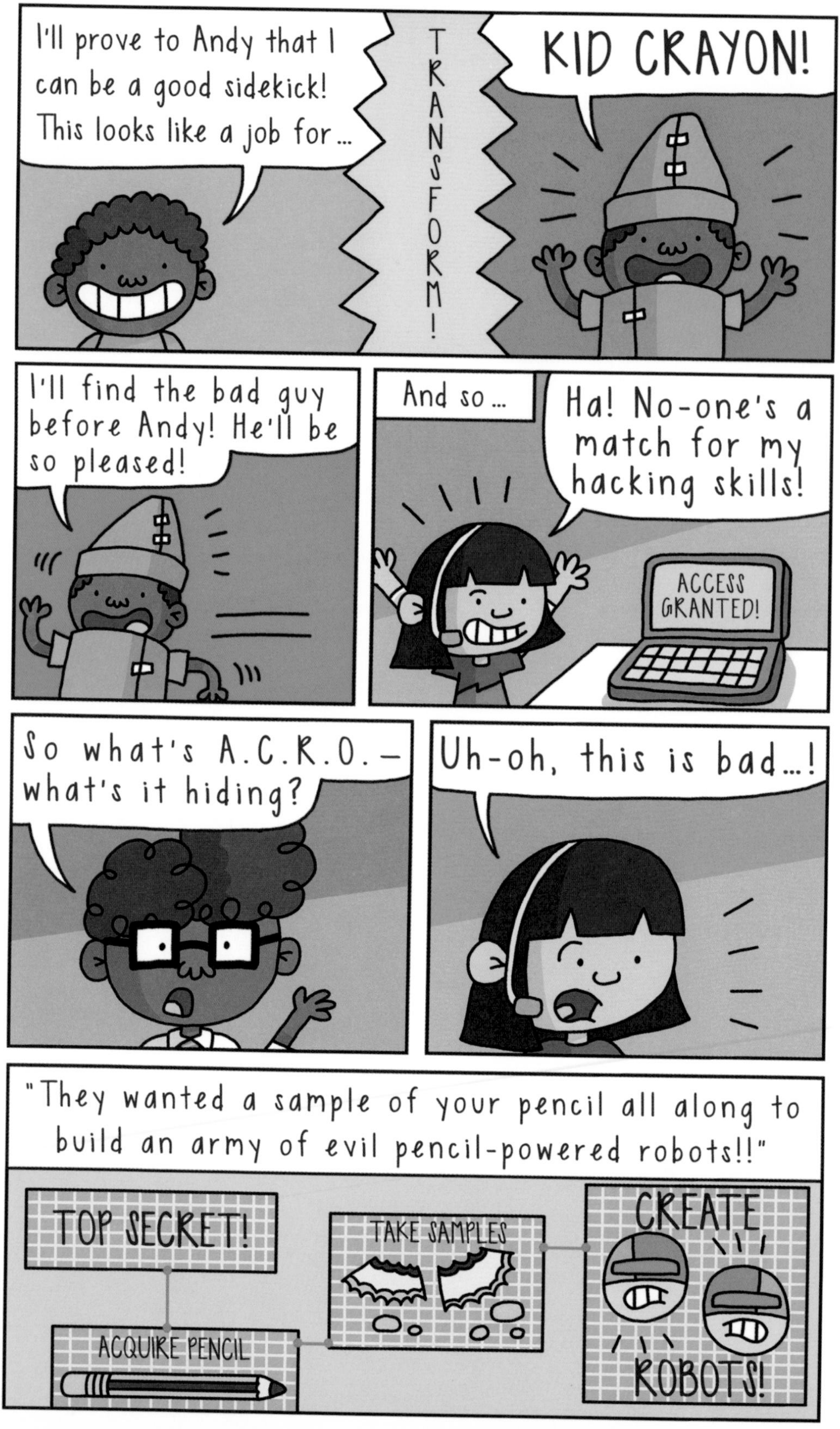

I'll prove to Andy that I can be a good sidekick! This looks like a job for ...
TRANSFORM!
KID CRAYON!
I'll find the bad guy before Andy! He'll be so pleased!
And so ...
Ha! No-one's a match for my hacking skills!
ACCESS GRANTED!
So what's A.C.R.O. – what's it hiding?
Uh-oh, this is bad...!
"They wanted a sample of your pencil all along to build an army of evil pencil-powered robots!!"
TOP SECRET!
ACQUIRE PENCIL
TAKE SAMPLES
CREATE
ROBOTS!

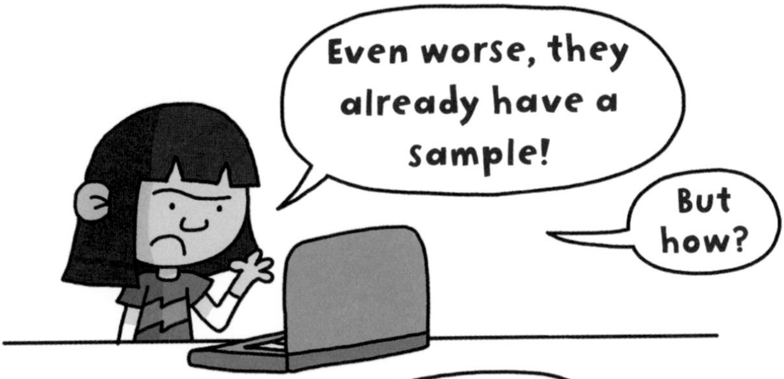
Even worse, they already have a sample!
But how?

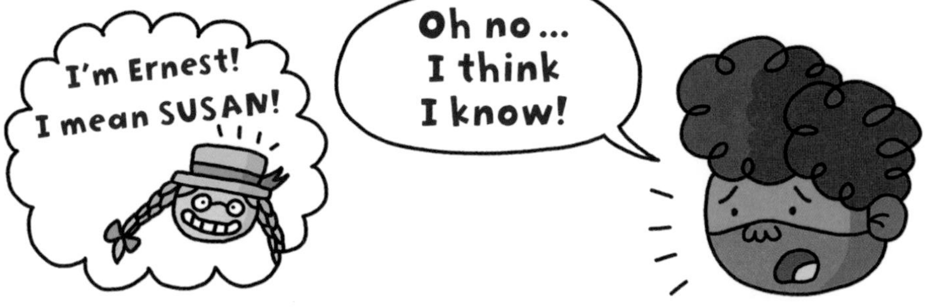
I'm Ernest! I mean SUSAN!
Oh no... I think I know!

"The sample must have become contaminated somehow and made him EVIL!" Mona said.

"Not only is the science of this really confusing me, but the one time I get a decent villain, it turns out that I created him!" I wailed.

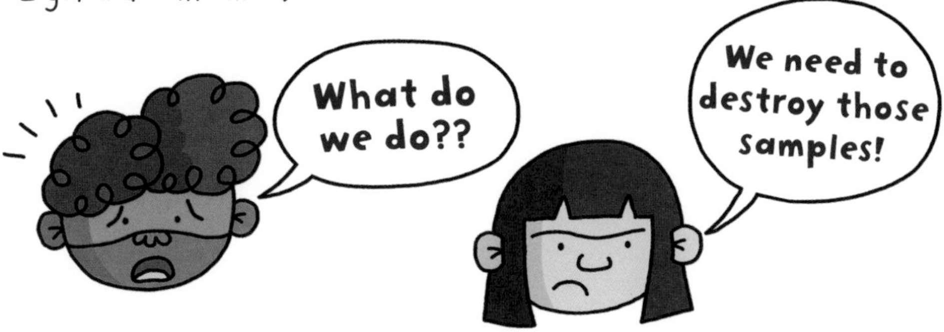
What do we do??
We need to destroy those samples!

"Okay, so we break into A.C.R.O.N.Y.M.'s highly secured HQ, find the samples, **destroy** them, get out, and then ACE tomorrow's test!" Mona said.

"EASY PEASY," I said, queasily.

"Look, I can hack into the security cameras AND download a floor plan, so yeah! Easy!" said Mona.

I grumbled in resignation.

"Let's just get into the security feed and see what we're up against!" Mona tapped away on her computer. "OH NO!" she groaned.

"What is it?" I asked.

"It's Oscar! He's at A.C.R.O.N.Y.M. dressed as a ... crayon?"

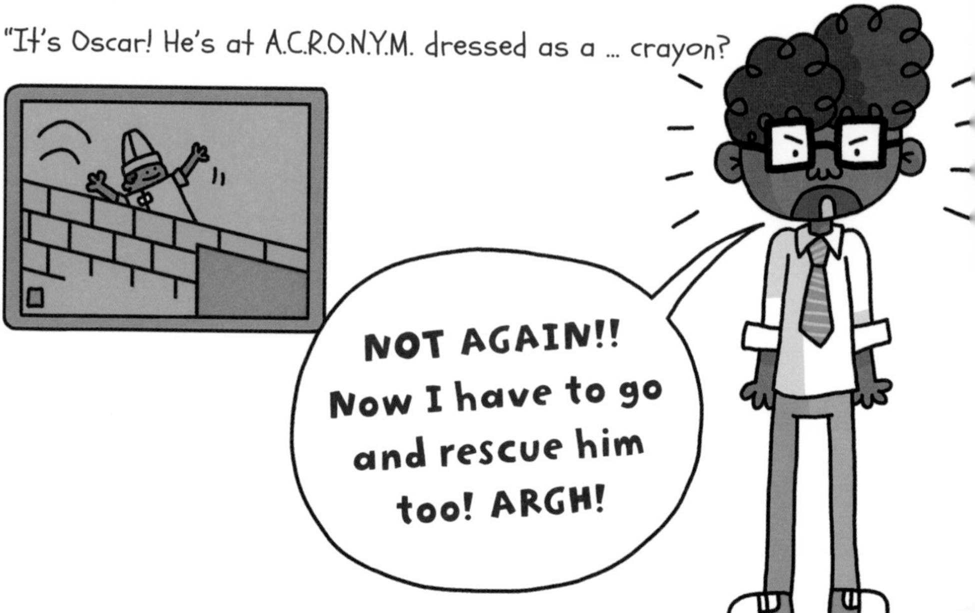
NOT AGAIN!! Now I have to go and rescue him too! ARGH!

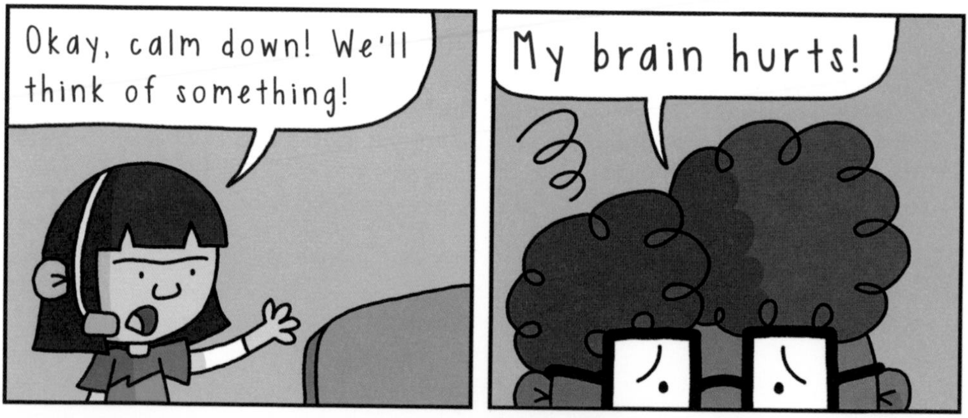
Okay, calm down! We'll think of something!
My brain hurts!

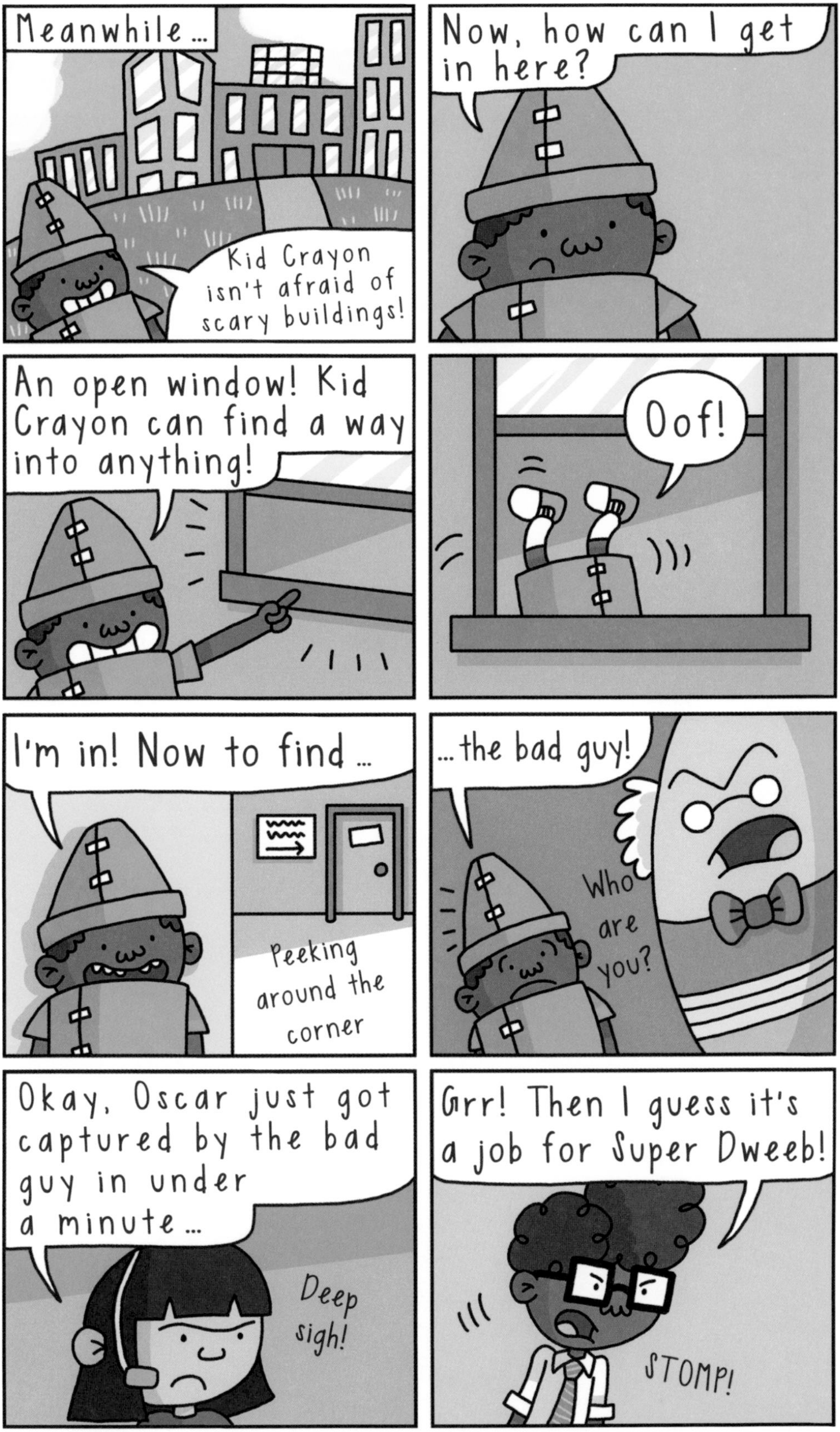
Meanwhile ...
Kid Crayon isn't afraid of scary buildings!
Now, how can I get in here?
An open window! Kid Crayon can find a way into anything!
Oof!
I'm in! Now to find ...
Peeking around the corner
... the bad guy!
Who are you?
Okay, Oscar just got captured by the bad guy in under a minute ...
Deep sigh!
Grr! Then I guess it's a job for Super Dweeb!
STOMP!

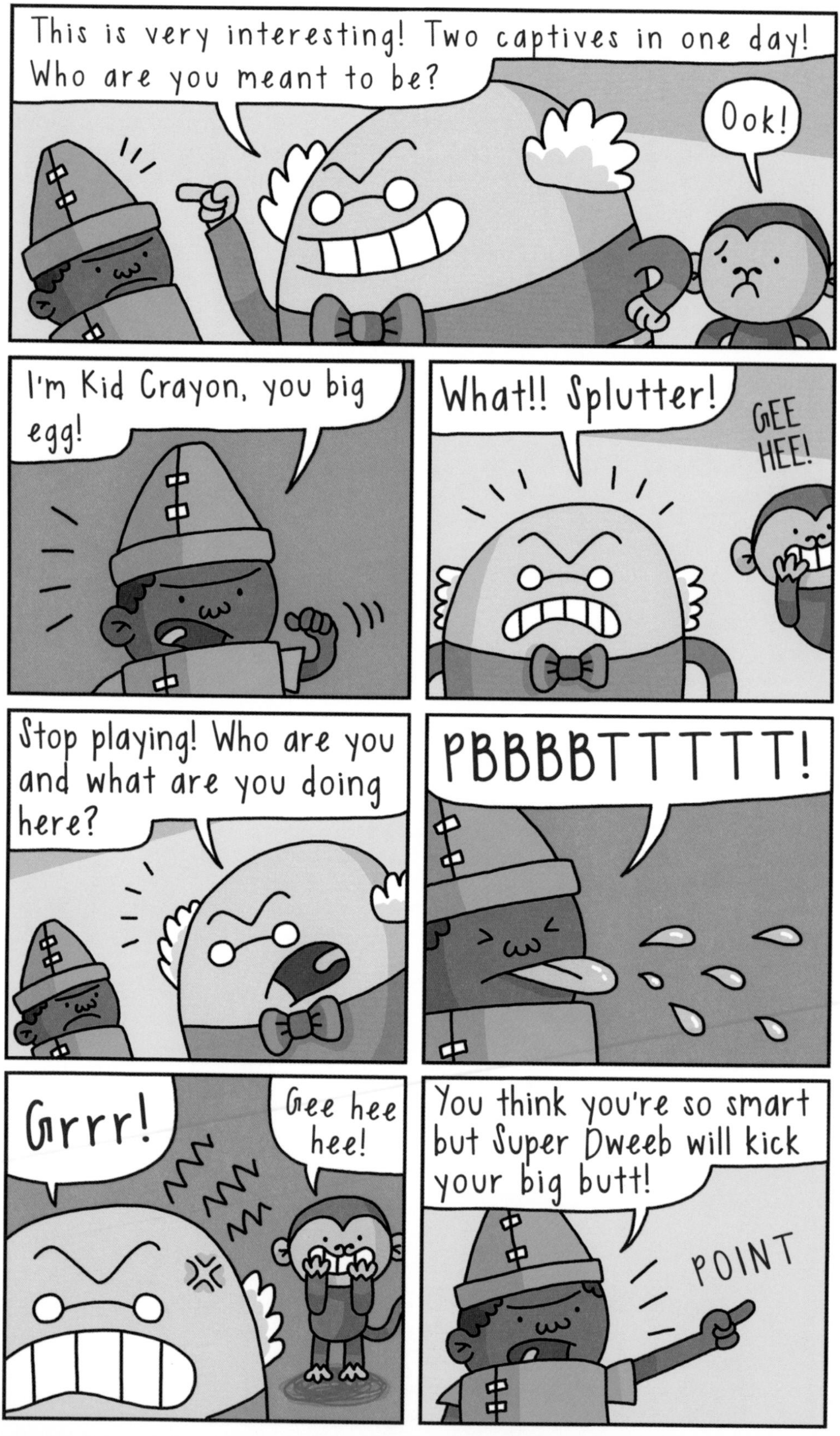
This is very interesting! Two captives in one day! Who are you meant to be?
Ook!
I'm Kid Crayon, you big egg!
What!! Splutter!
GEE HEE!
Stop playing! Who are you and what are you doing here?
PBBBBTTTTT!
Grrr!
Gee hee hee!
You think you're so smart but Super Dweeb will kick your big butt!
POINT

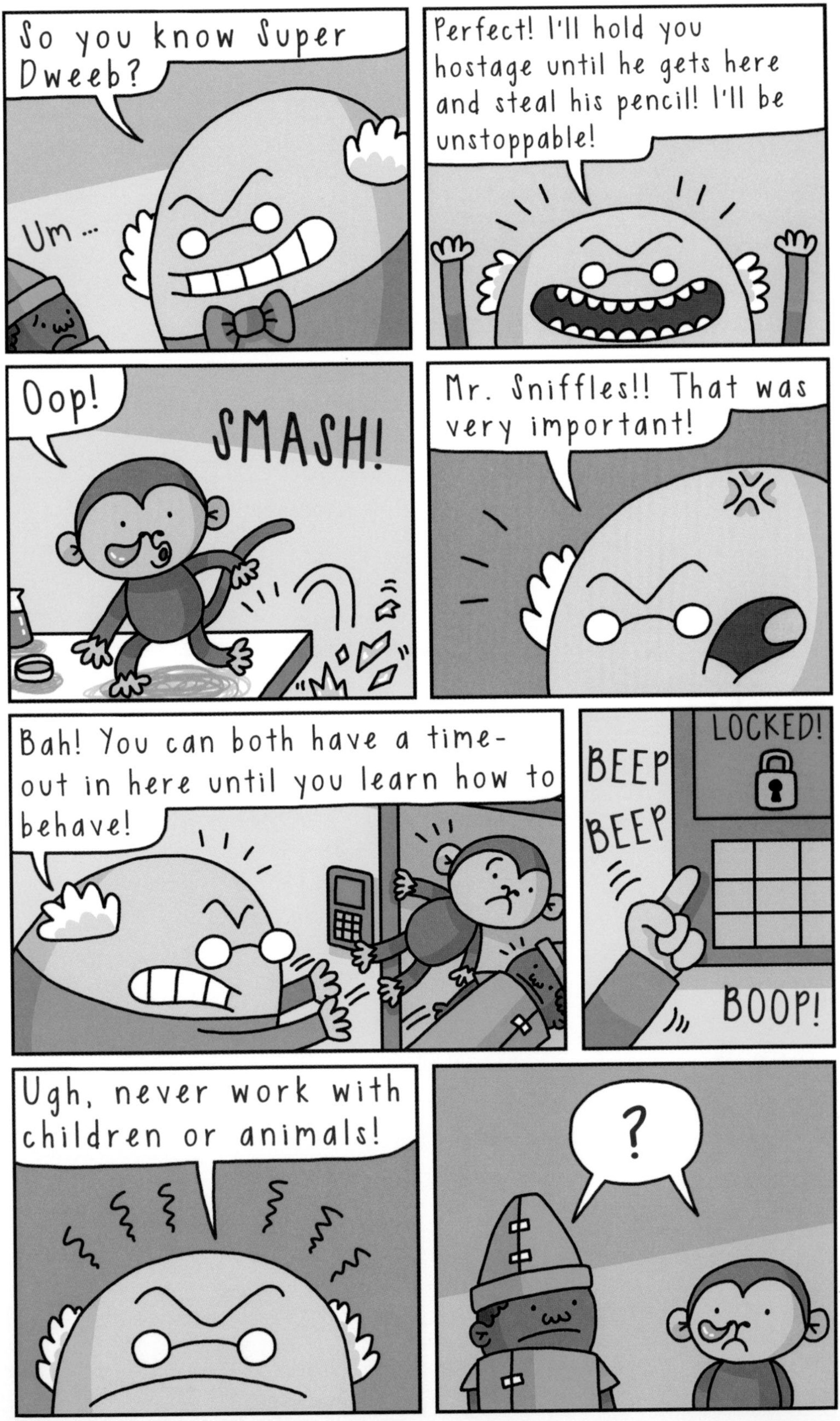
So you know Super Dweeb?
Um ...
Perfect! I'll hold you hostage until he gets here and steal his pencil! I'll be unstoppable!
Oop!
SMASH!
Mr. Sniffles!! That was very important!
Bah! You can both have a time-out in here until you learn how to behave!
BEEP
BEEP
LOCKED!
BOOP!
Ugh, never work with children or animals!
?

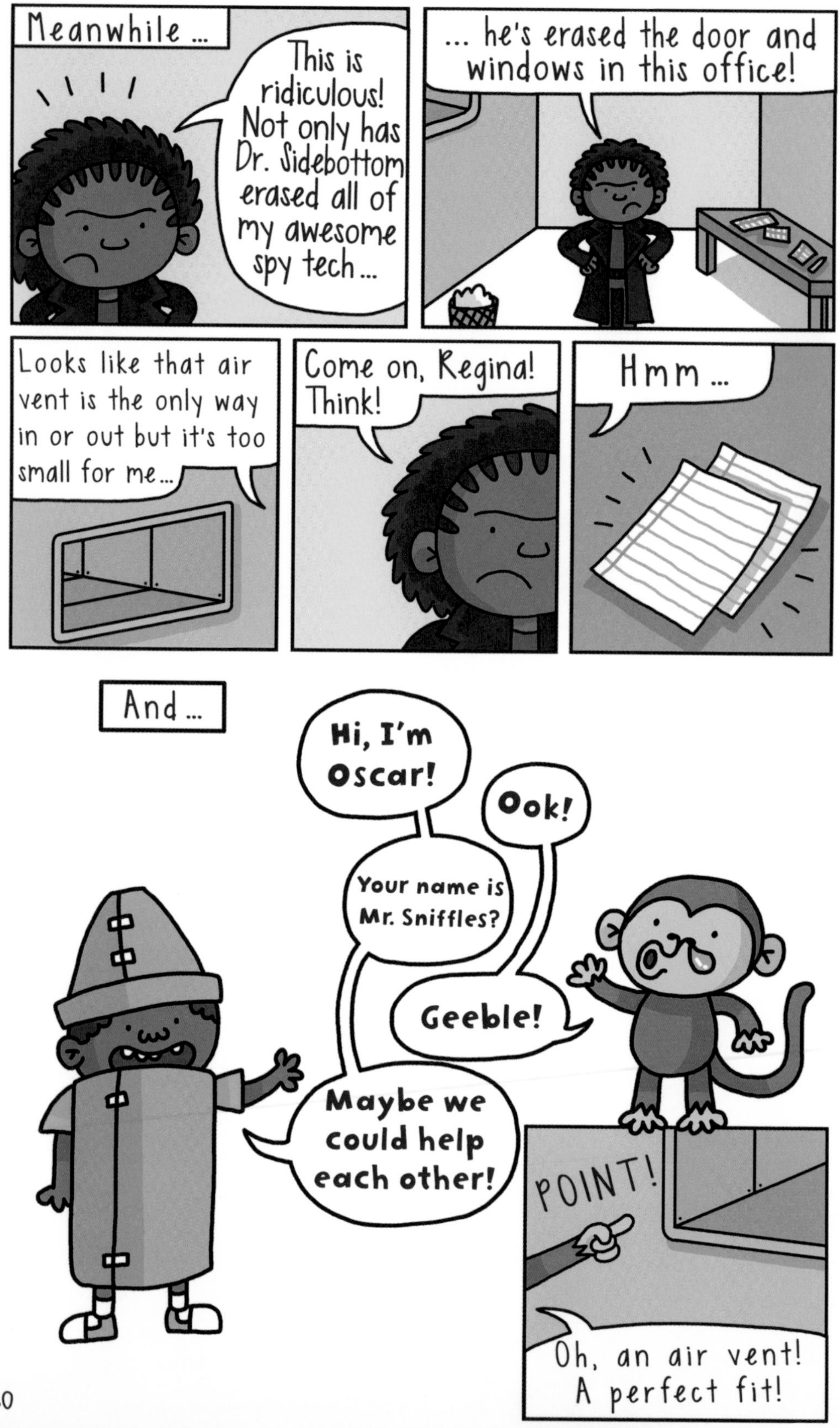
Meanwhile ...
This is ridiculous! Not only has Dr. Sidebottom erased all of my awesome spy tech ...
... he's erased the door and windows in this office!
Looks like that air vent is the only way in or out but it's too small for me...
Come on, Regina! Think!
Hmm ...
And ...
Hi, I'm Oscar!
Ook!
Your name is Mr. Sniffles?
Geeble!
Maybe we could help each other!
POINT!
Oh, an air vent! A perfect fit!

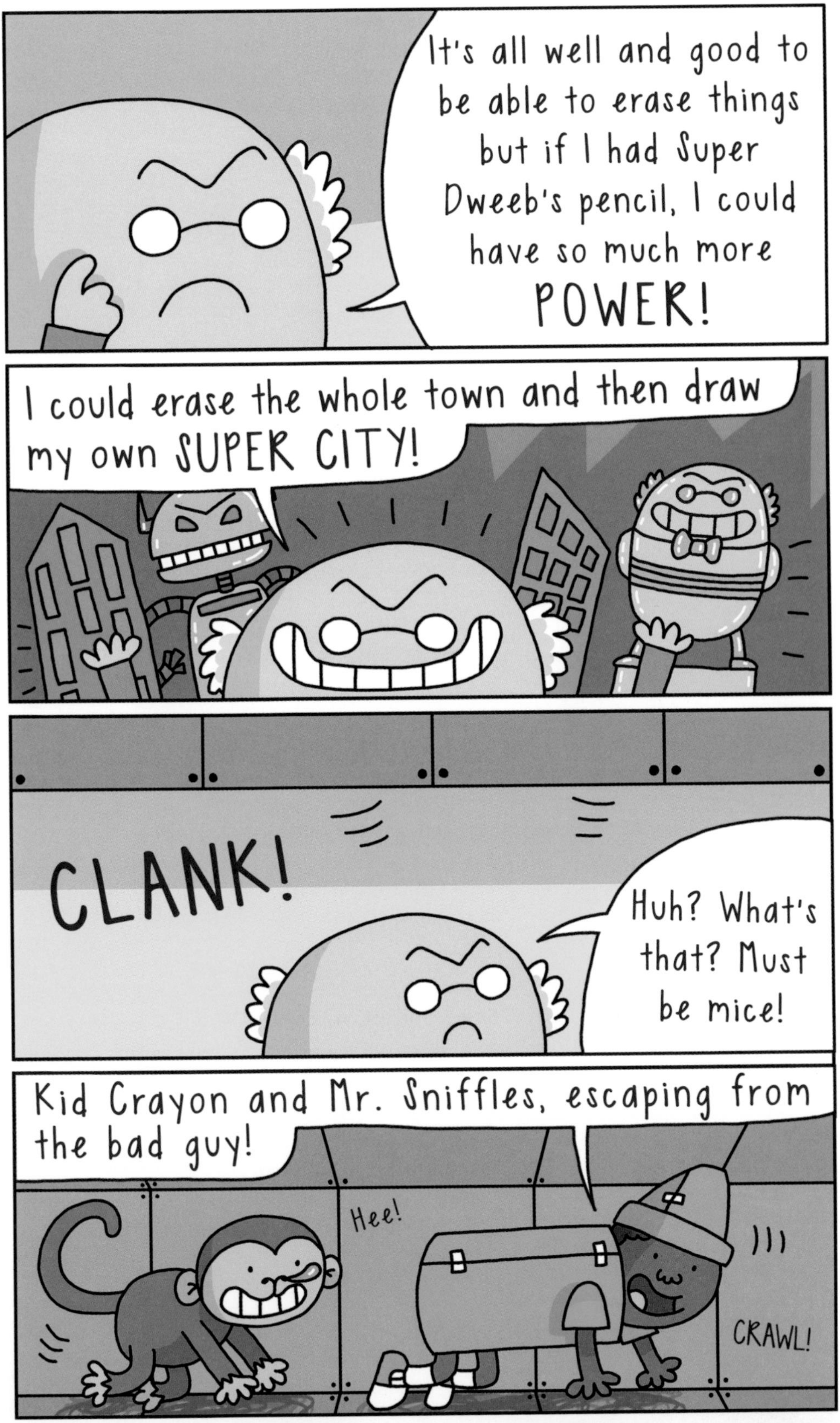
It's all well and good to be able to erase things but if I had Super Dweeb's pencil, I could have so much more POWER!
I could erase the whole town and then draw my own SUPER CITY!
CLANK!
Huh? What's that? Must be mice!
Kid Crayon and Mr. Sniffles, escaping from the bad guy!
Hee!
CRAWL!

Okay, now all I had to do was sneak out of here before

my parents noticed...

KNOCK KNOCK!

"Andy?" Mom called.

"Erk! Yes?" I squeaked.

"Dad and I are going to a P.T.A. MEETING so Amy

is here to babysit. Is Oscar with you?"

"Um, yes! He's playing the quiet game!" I said.

Mona snorted through my earpiece. "SMOOTH!"

"When you've finished studying, put Oscar to bed, okay?"

"Sure, Mom. See you later!" I waited until I heard the

front door close. "Phew! What a stroke of luck!"

Amy won't come in here and I'll just draw a decoy
Andy and Oscar and leave them a box of pencils to
munch on!

SCRIBBLE!

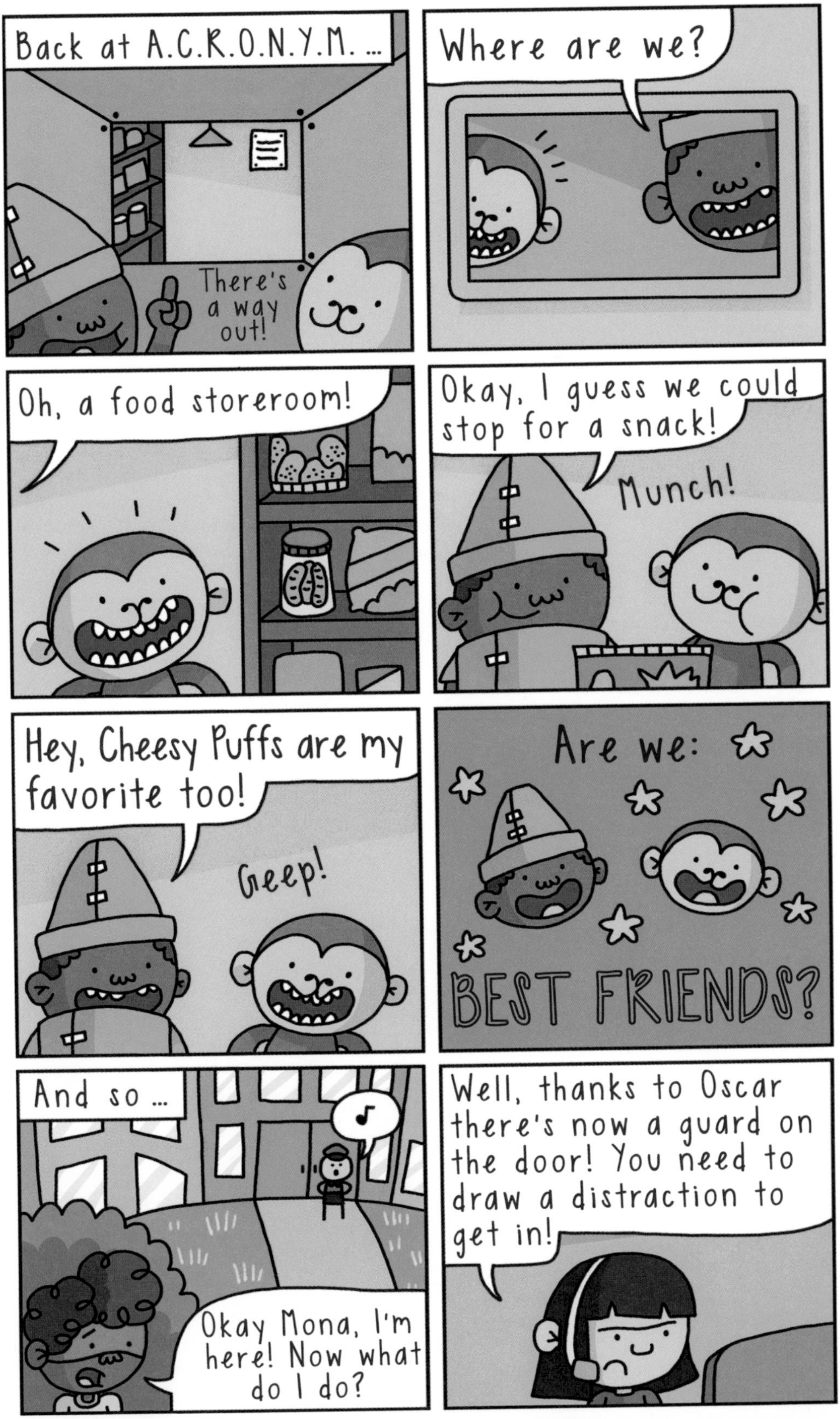

Back at A.C.R.O.N.Y.M. ...
There's a way out!
Where are we?
Oh, a food storeroom!
Okay, I guess we could stop for a snack!
Munch!
Hey, Cheesy Puffs are my favorite too!
Geep!
Are we:
BEST FRIENDS?
And so ...
Okay Mona, I'm here! Now what do I do?
Well, thanks to Oscar there's now a guard on the door! You need to draw a distraction to get in!

"I can do better than that!" I said. "I'll draw a distraction that will distract the entire **BUILDING!**"

"GOOD IDEA," said Mona. "If we can cause enough chaos, no-one will notice you sneaking around!"

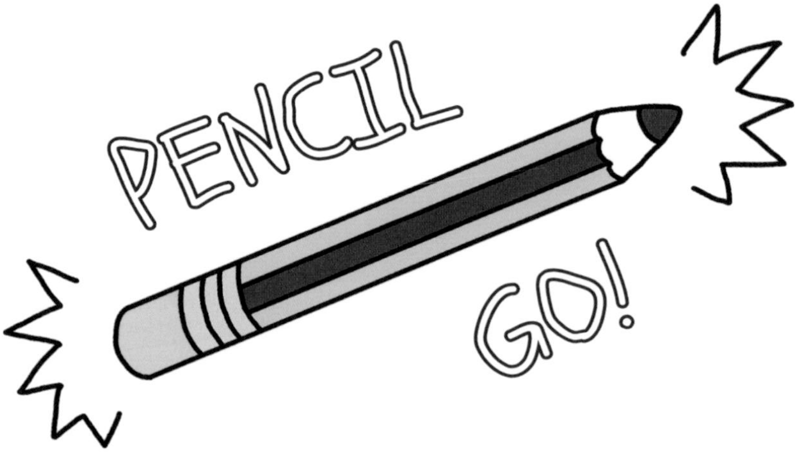
PENCIL
GO!

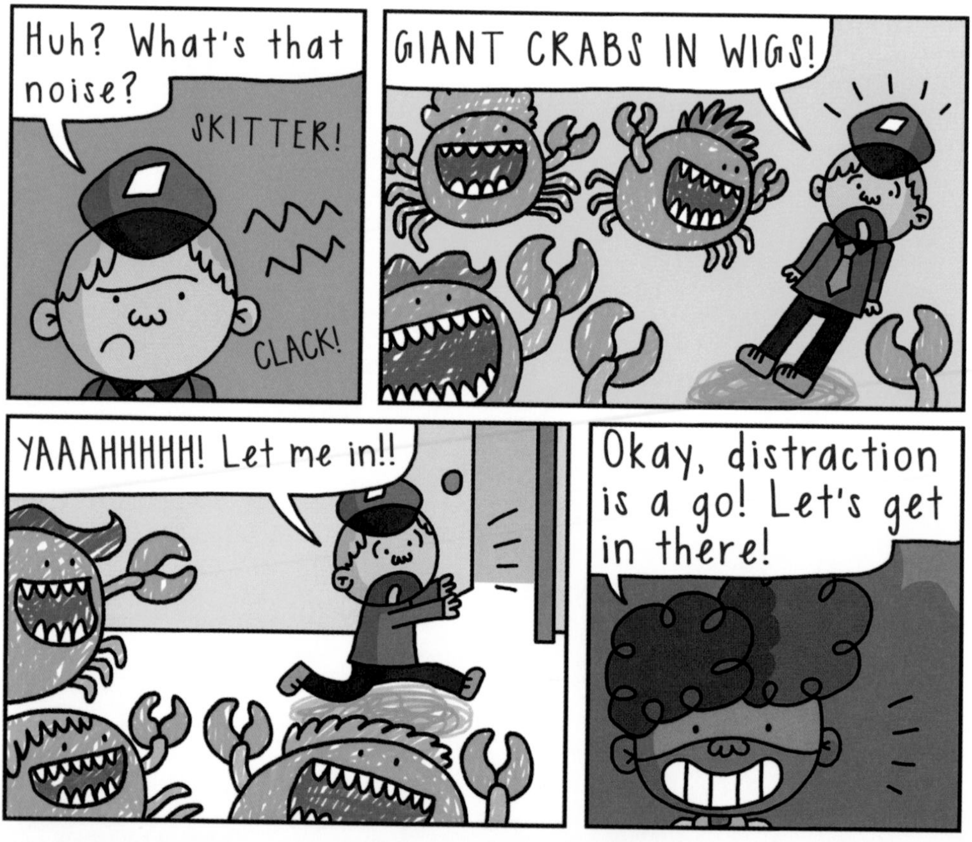
Huh? What's that noise?
SKITTER!
CLACK!
GIANT CRABS IN WIGS!
YAAAHHHHH! Let me in!!
Okay, distraction is a go! Let's get in there!

Chapter 7 **Team-Up Time**

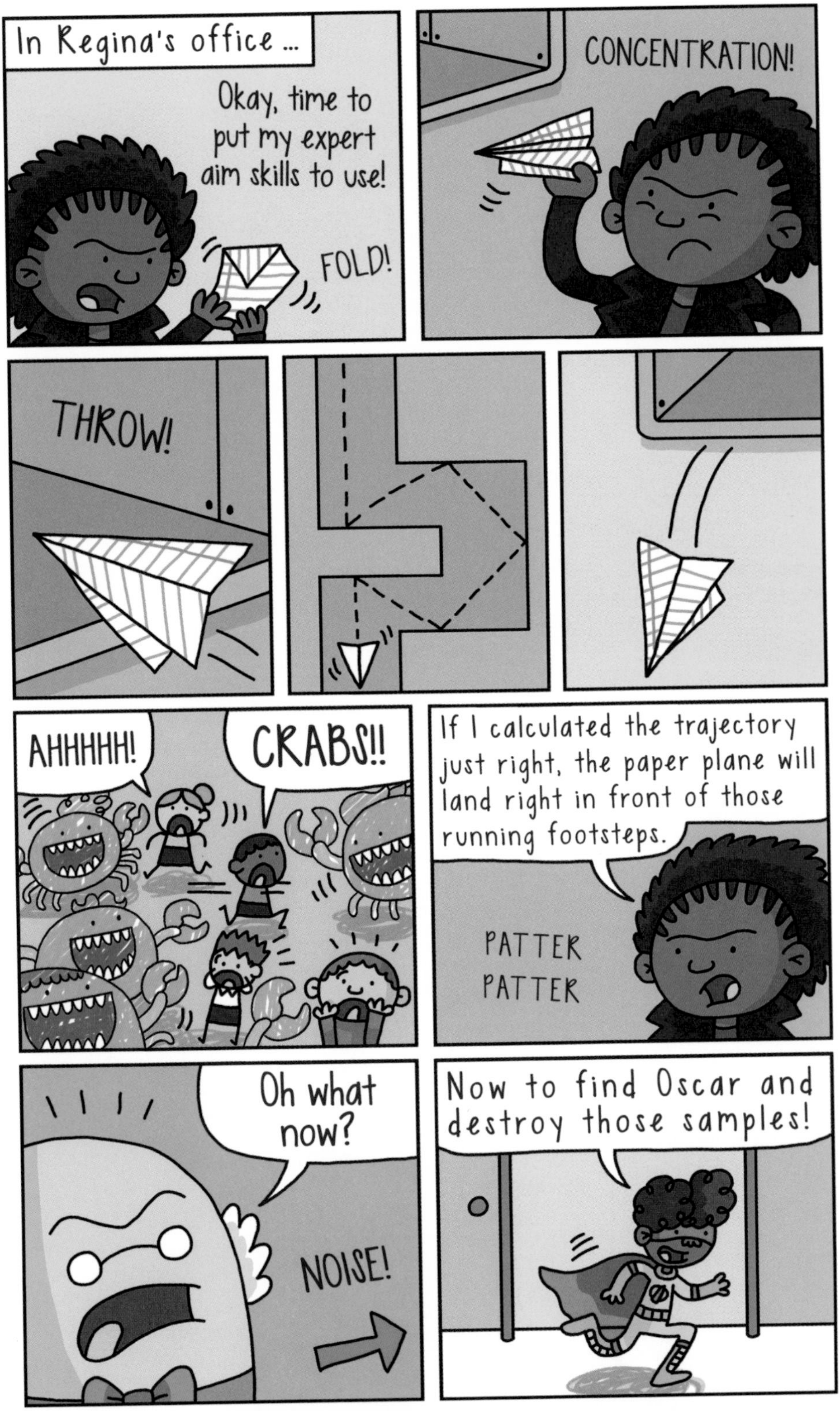
In Regina's office ...
Okay, time to put my expert aim skills to use!
FOLD!
CONCENTRATION!
THROW!
AHHHHH!
CRABS!!
If I calculated the trajectory just right, the paper plane will land right in front of those running footsteps.
PATTER PATTER
Oh what now?
NOISE!
Now to find Oscar and destroy those samples!

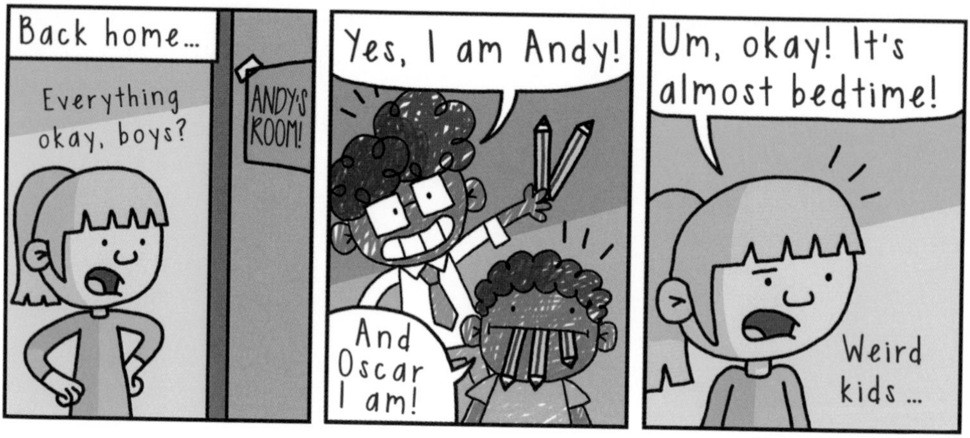
Back home...
Everything okay, boys?
ANDY'S ROOM!
Yes, I am Andy!
And Oscar I am!
Um, okay! It's almost bedtime!
Weird kids ...

As I ran down the corridor trying to find Oscar, I saw a paper plane land on the floor.

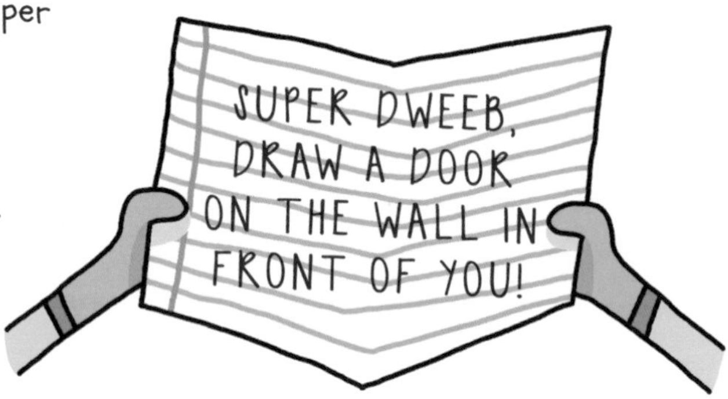
SUPER DWEEB, DRAW A DOOR ON THE WALL IN FRONT OF YOU!

"Hey, what's this?" I said.

"Stop wasting time!" Mona said.

I opened the plane. "Oh, it's a letter!"

"Well, I can do that!" I said and drew a door on the wall with my pencil.

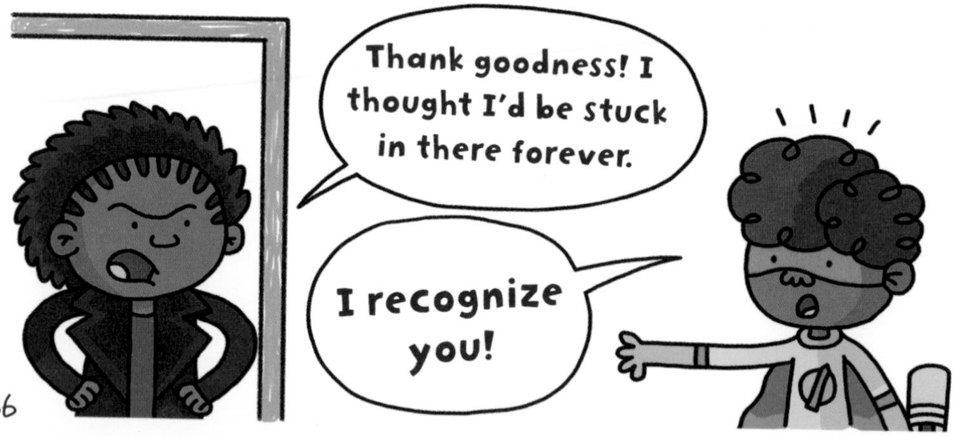
Thank goodness! I thought I'd be stuck in there forever.
I recognize you!

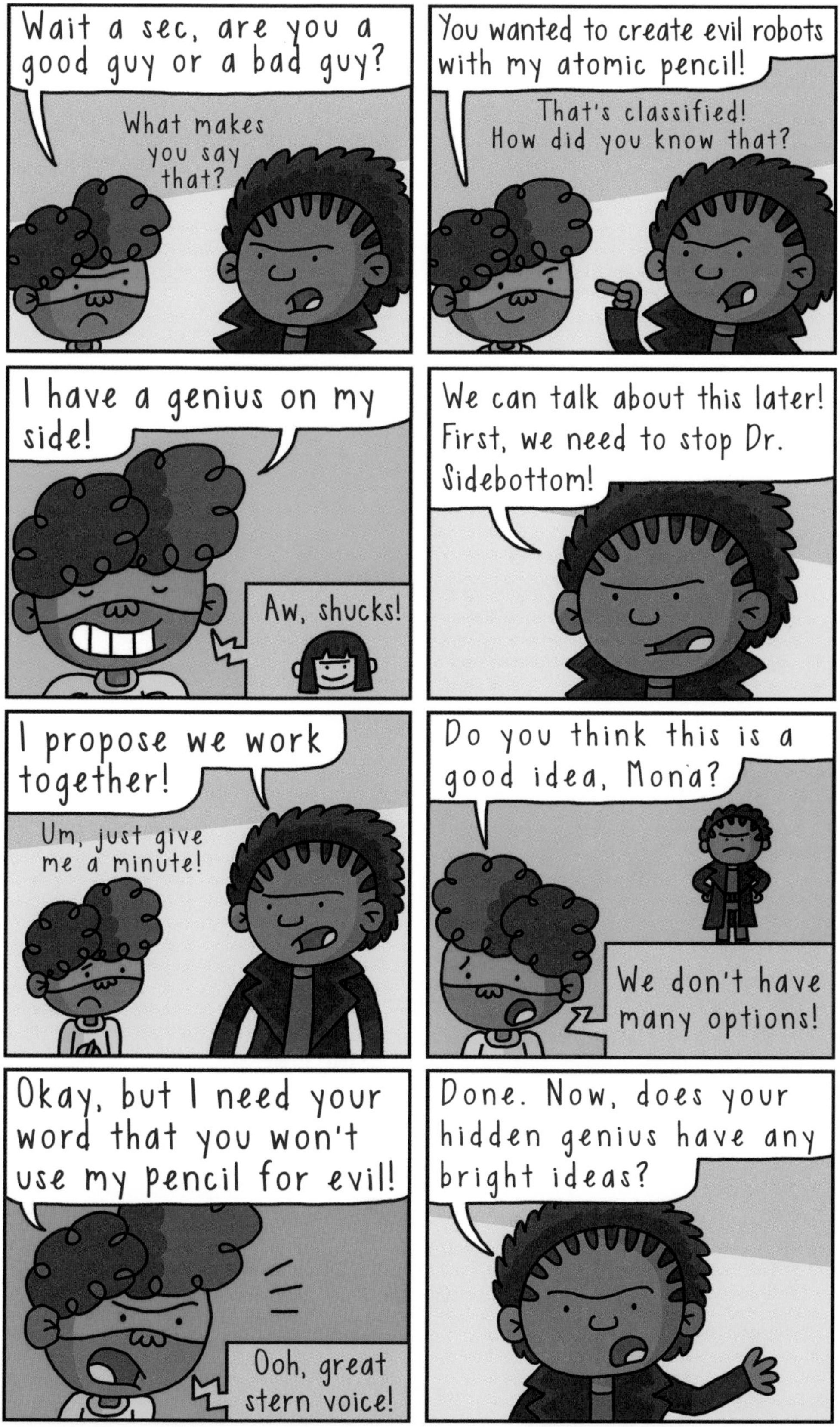

Wait a sec, are you a good guy or a bad guy?
What makes you say that?
You wanted to create evil robots with my atomic pencil!
That's classified! How did you know that?
I have a genius on my side!
Aw, shucks!
We can talk about this later! First, we need to stop Dr. Sidebottom!
I propose we work together!
Um, just give me a minute!
Do you think this is a good idea, Mona?
We don't have many options!
Okay, but I need your word that you won't use my pencil for evil!
Ooh, great stern voice!
Done. Now, does your hidden genius have any bright ideas?

"I do," said Mona over my earpiece. "THE ONLY WAY TO STOP DR. ERASER-BUTT IS TO ERASE ..."

There was an awkward silence.

"Um, are you still there?" I asked.

Mona sighed. "That was a dramatic pause."

"Oh, sorry!" I said. "Carry on."

"You need to erase HIS BUTT."

I grinned. "Erase the eraser! We just need to get close enough to erase it!"

Erase his butt?

It's the source of his power!

Hmpf. Smart kids!

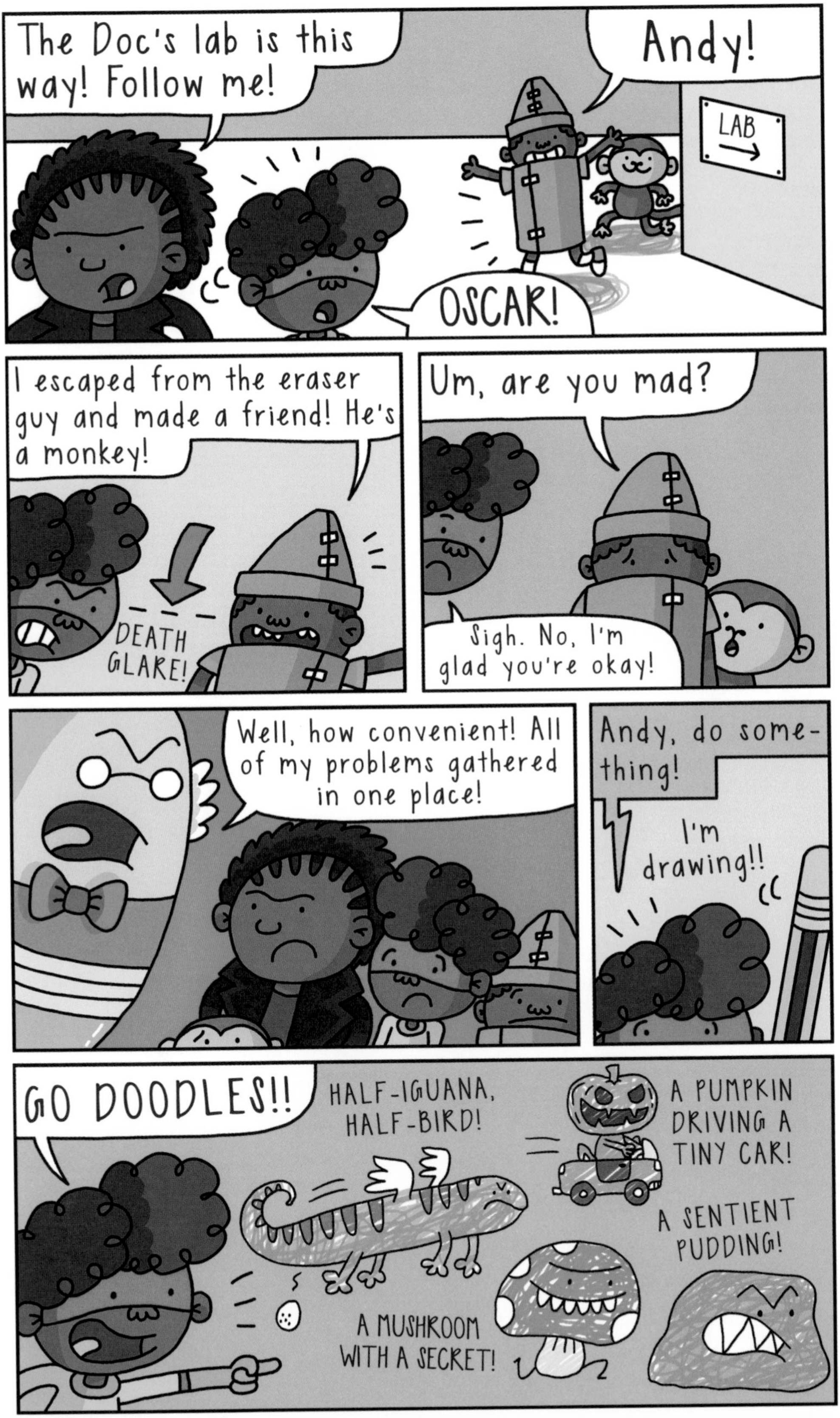
The Doc's lab is this way! Follow me!
Andy!
LAB
OSCAR!
I escaped from the eraser guy and made a friend! He's a monkey!
DEATH GLARE!
Um, are you mad?
Sigh. No, I'm glad you're okay!
Well, how convenient! All of my problems gathered in one place!
Andy, do something!
I'm drawing!!
GO DOODLES!!
HALF-IGUANA, HALF-BIRD!
A PUMPKIN DRIVING A TINY CAR!
A SENTIENT PUDDING!
A MUSHROOM WITH A SECRET!

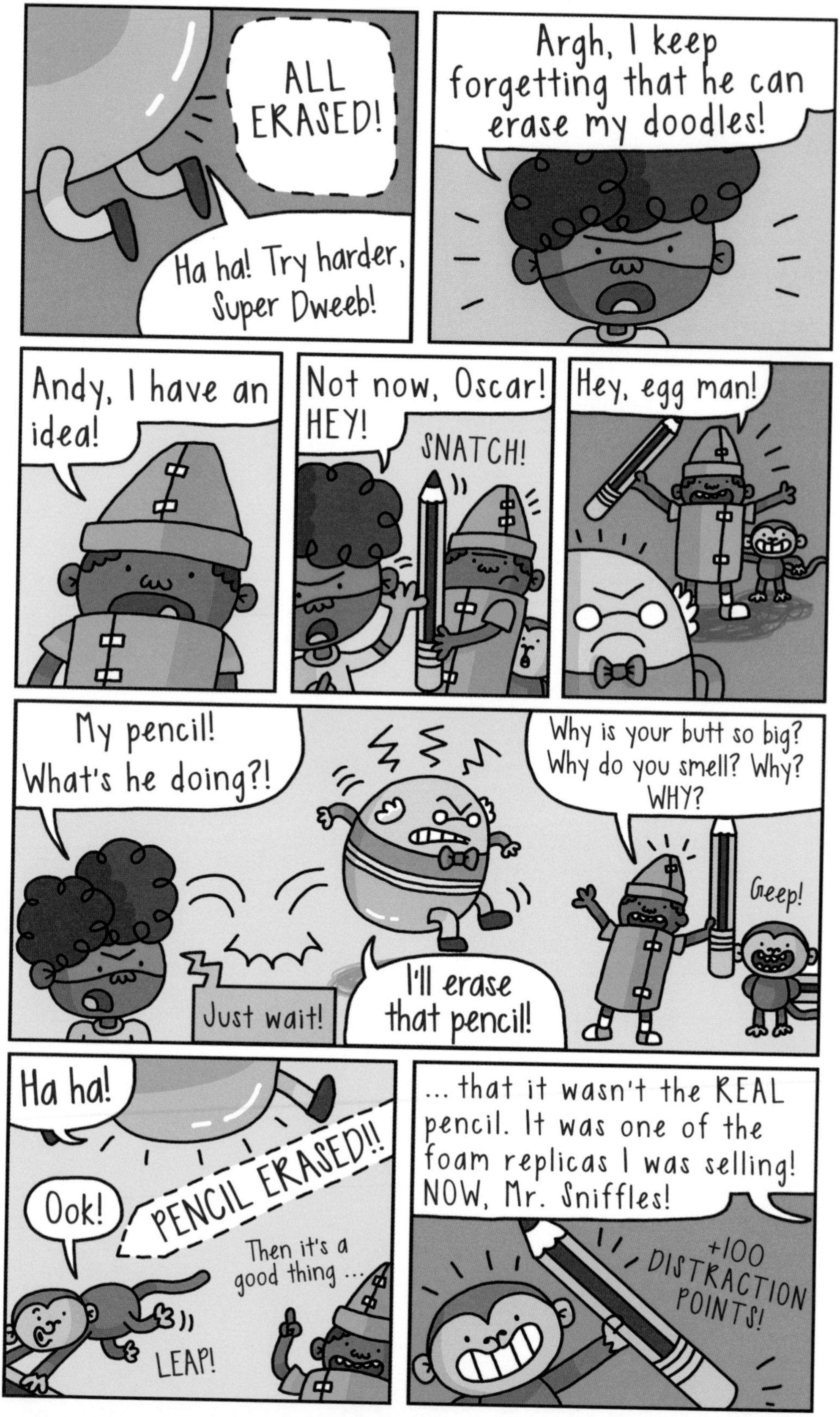
ALL ERASED!
Ha ha! Try harder, Super Dweeb!
Argh, I keep forgetting that he can erase my doodles!
Andy, I have an idea!
Not now, Oscar! HEY!
SNATCH!
Hey, egg man!
My pencil! What's he doing?!
Why is your butt so big? Why do you smell? Why? WHY?
Geep!
Just wait!
I'll erase that pencil!
Ha ha!
PENCIL ERASED!!
Ook!
Then it's a good thing ...
LEAP!
... that it wasn't the REAL pencil. It was one of the foam replicas I was selling! NOW, Mr. Sniffles!
+100 DISTRACTION POINTS!

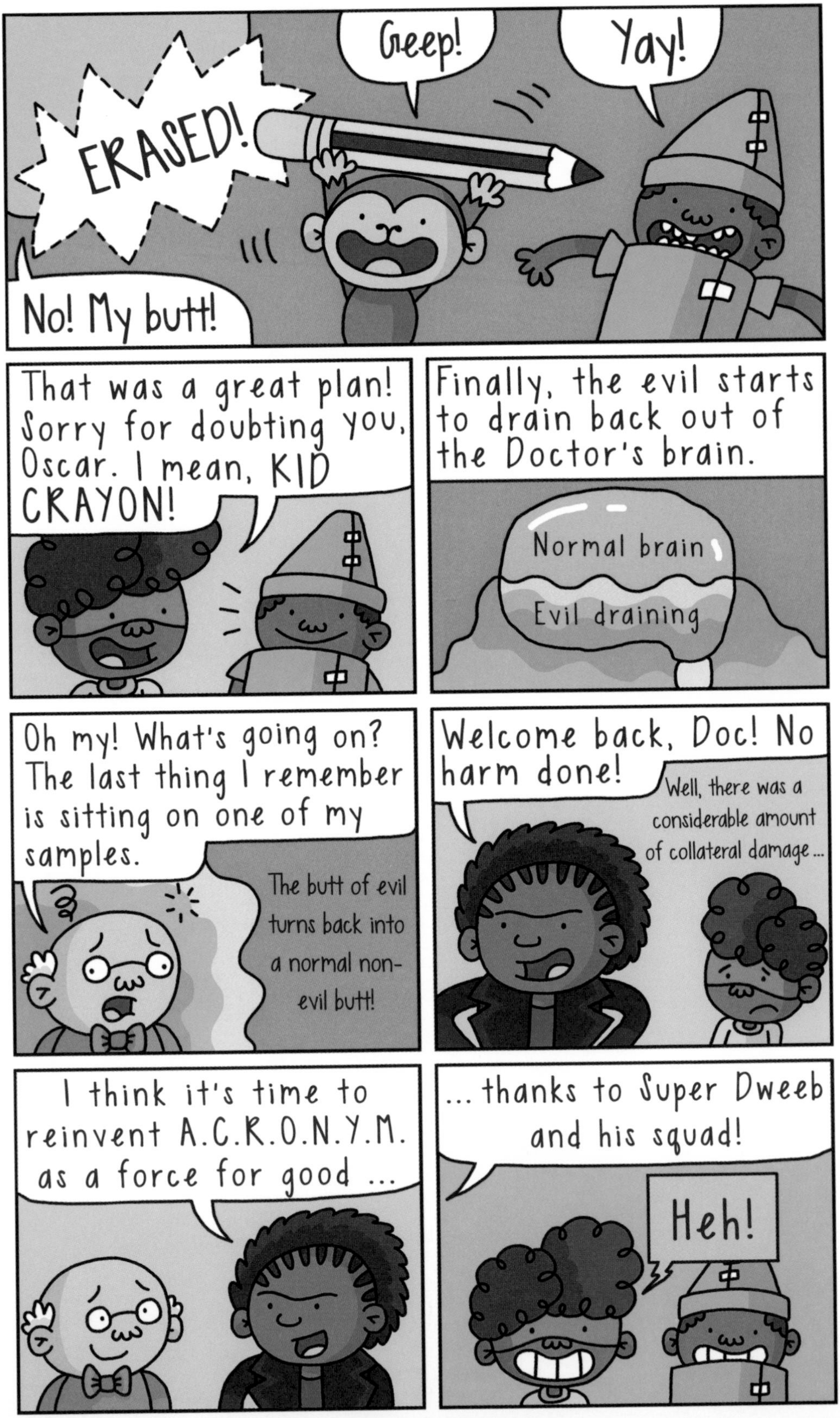
ERASED!
Geep!
Yay!
No! My butt!
That was a great plan! Sorry for doubting you, Oscar. I mean, KID CRAYON!
Finally, the evil starts to drain back out of the Doctor's brain.
Normal brain
Evil draining
Oh my! What's going on? The last thing I remember is sitting on one of my samples.
The butt of evil turns back into a normal non-evil butt!
Welcome back, Doc! No harm done!
Well, there was a considerable amount of collateral damage ...
I think it's time to reinvent A.C.R.O.N.Y.M. as a force for good ...
... thanks to Super Dweeb and his squad!
Heh!

Chapter 8 **Back at Dweeb HQ**

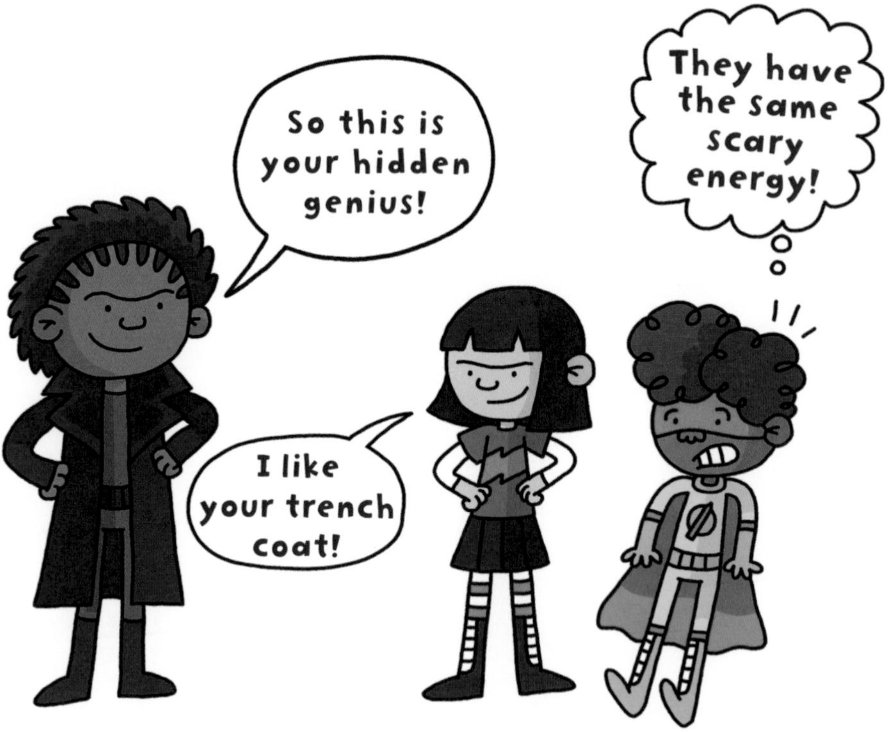
So this is your hidden genius!
They have the same scary energy!
I like your trench coat!

"So thanks to all of you, the pencil samples have been destroyed and WE'RE OVERHAULING ALL OF A.C.R.O.N.Y.M.

"No more unstoppable cyborg armies!" said Agent Storm.

"PHEW!" I said.

"Maybe A.C.R.O.N.Y.M. could help us in the future," Mona said.

Agent Storm raised an eyebrow. "Maybe. And maybe we'll have some summer internships available too!"

I'm not sure the world is ready for Mona AND Agent Storm!

Agent Storm waved and left. "See you around!"

"Phew, what a day!" I said.

"Come on," said Mona. "We can squeeze in some last minute studying!"

I sighed. "Fine! We need to get home before Mom and Dad do but I'll speak to you later?"

"You know it!" Mona said.

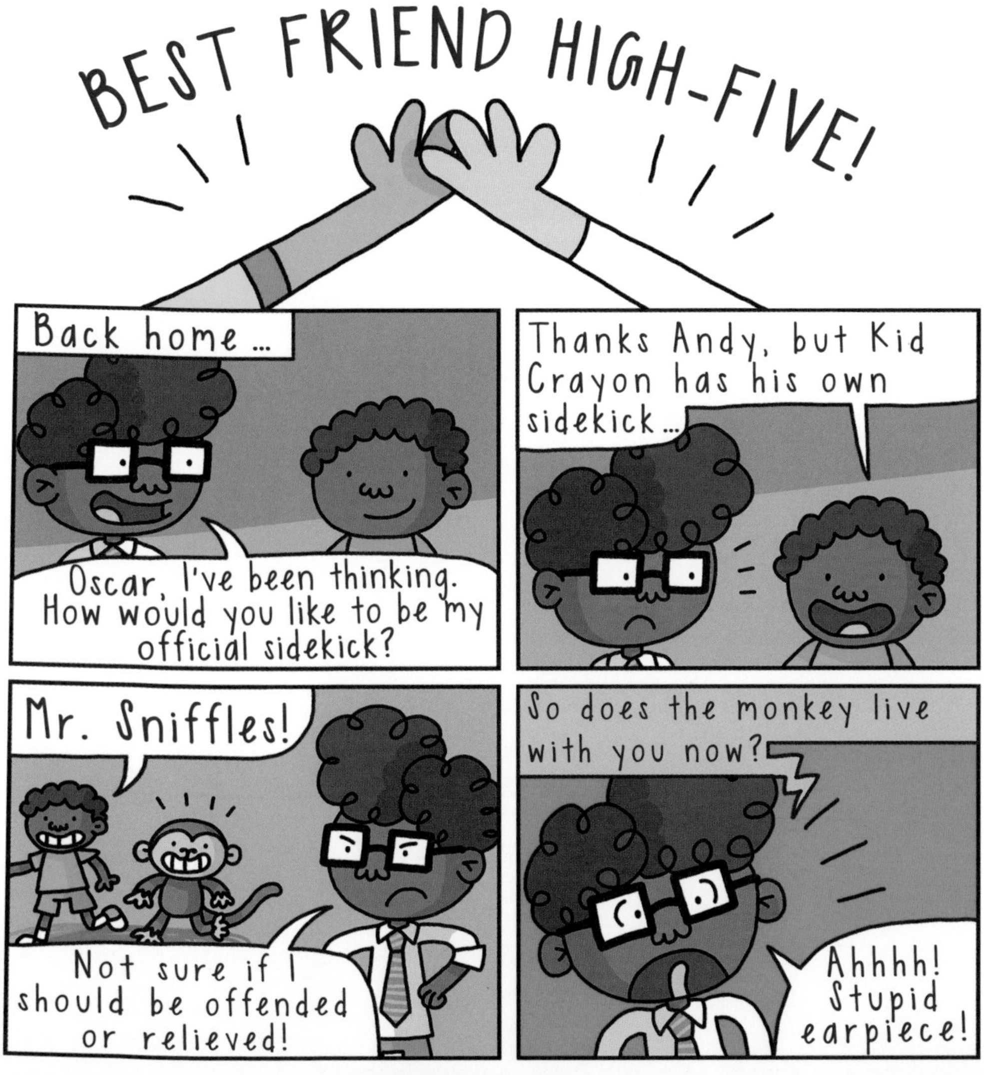
BEST FRIEND HIGH-FIVE!
Back home ...
Oscar, I've been thinking. How would you like to be my official sidekick?
Thanks Andy, but Kid Crayon has his own sidekick ...
Mr. Sniffles!
Not sure if I should be offended or relieved!
So does the monkey live with you now?
Ahhhh! Stupid earpiece!

Andy's new report card

Test score: 96/100

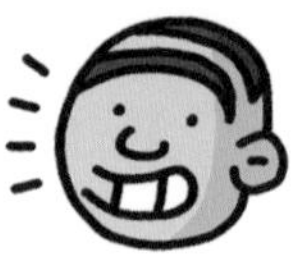

Mr. Squibb says: Andy's work has improved so much that I no longer think he is a pod person. Well done!

So everything pretty much worked out! I ACED MY TEST. Now I'm studying hard to get my grades back up and not letting my Andy-matter decoys do my homework! I've also learned that it can be **hard** to get the right balance between being a KID and a SUPERHERO.

Luckily, my amazing best friend Mona has my back for being a kid AND a superhero!
Told you my tutoring skills would get you an A!
Yeah, yeah!
And whatever happens, we know that the city will always be safe from evil, thanks to ... Kid Crayon and Mr. Sniffles!
HEY!!
FIN!

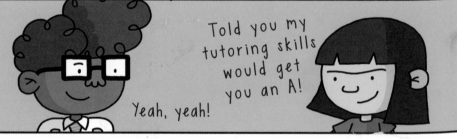

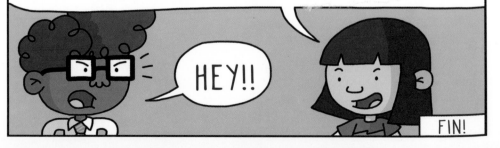